The Drunken Promise
A Steamy Romance Novella
By Max Watson

Max Watson Books LLC

Max Watson Books LLC
PO Box 821641
Dallas, TX 75382
www.MaxWatsonBooks.com

Second edition December 2020

Max Watson Books LLC and colophon are trademarks of Max Watson Books LLC

To book an event, contact the publisher, request an interview with the author and more contact Max Watson Books LLC at PO Box 821641 Dallas, TX 75382 or visit our website at www.MaxWatsonBooks.com.

Cover design by Sarah Kil Creative Studio
ISBN Print: 978-1-7340197-4-2
ISBN eBook: 978-1-7340197-5-9
PREVIOUSLY PUBLISHED AS BLACK & BLUE ISBNs:
978-1-7340197-3-5 (print); 978-1-7340197-2-8 (ebook)

The Drunken Promise

1. Angel

Hi, Daddy. It's me, your Angel. I'm your daughter. I'll be turning thirteen soon. Mom jokes that you're so lucky you don't get to see me turn into a teenage monster. I don't think I'll turn into those pizza-face weirdos you see on TV. I'll be a nice teenager. And all the adults will say what a nice example I make or something.

Today was career day at school. They told us a bunch of doctors, lawyers, and firefighters would come in to tell us about their jobs. Then everyone had a family member come in but none of them had any cool jobs like that. Most of them worked in factories. One did something called a freelancer. It made me think of horses and long sticks and doing it for free but calling it work. But they said they worked at home, like their bosses never made them come in and they could do everything online. That sounds pretty cool.

At the end of the day, we had to write what we want to do when we grow up. I said doctor because I thought it was funny since nobody's parents were doctors but I think I might like to actually be one. If I'm a doctor I can teach you how to walk and talk again. And we can play on the playground again. You remember that train game where me, you, and mommy would all go down the slide together? I wanna do that again once I fix you.

Mom says I shouldn't talk about your injuries in my letters to you but my teacher says you should look for the light no matter how dark it gets. She says that means to have hope. So I'm gonna hope I'll become a doctor someday and be good enough to fix you. My friends say it's stupid to pick a career just 'cause I wanna play with you again. They said I won't want to play once I'm old enough to be a doctor. But I don't care if I'm fifty and you're one hundred, I wanna play again someday.

I guess you're not that old. I saw something online about a woman who was like 125 or something and you don't look that old. Just sad. I came to see you today when they were trying to get you to talk. It looked like you just wanted to sleep forever and wished they would leave you alone. I don't think you know who I am so that's why I'm telling you all this boring stuff. Mom says you know and can understand what I say but I don't know.

Mom doesn't know I'm writing this late. I'm hiding under my blankets with my phone for light writing this by hand. I know, old-fashioned, huh? I could just email all this to you instead of writing it down. My hand already hurts. You know we don't really ever write on paper in school so I think writing letters by hand is kinda fun and old-fashioned. Oh, I said that already. That's the only thing that sucks is you can't erase anything. Sorry for all the scribbles, it's hard to remember how to spell sometimes without autocorrect. I have to keep looking up how to spell words on my phone then scribbling and rewriting. Hopefully you can still read this. Well, once I become a doctor and teach you how to read again.

I should go to bed. My hand is cramping. I love you, Daddy. Don't look so sad, I'll grow up and fix you real soon, 'kay?

Love, Angel

2. Black and Blue

My favorite fantasy about Blue is based off a dream I had once. I dreamt she tapped on my window and lured me outside. Then suddenly we were swimming, skinny dipping, in the moonlight. In my dream, nothing really happens. But that following morning, all I could see when I closed my eyes was her glistening wet body streaked silver by the light of the moon.

The fantasy is a lot more advanced and X-rated than my innocent dream of forever ago. I like to start slow, build up the tension. While the water in my shower warms up to that perfect temperature, we're slowly undressing, eyes glued to each other. And when I absentmindedly massage shampoo into my hair, I'm holding my breath at the bottom of the pool, watching her swim circles around me. Her legs open and close right over my head as she soars passed.

Just when the fantasy is really starting to get interesting, a loud thud reverberates through the house. I pause to listen, straining under the roar of the shower. Is that yelling I hear? For a moment I think I might get to hear my parents argue for the first time, but then there's nothing but silence. With a shrug, I dive back into the cool pool of my fantasy. Blue tackles me beneath the water, our slick bodies sliding together as we swim for the surface, wrapped around each other.

A rush of cold air stirs the steam of the shower as the door clangs open. Just when I open my mouth to yell at whoever thinks they can come in here and stink up the place in the middle of my shower, the curtain is ripped aside. A schoolgirl scream lodges in my throat and I nearly fold myself up to cover my nakedness. Thick black curls blur before my eyes and then Blue's there, standing in my shower, clinging to me.

"What the—" I grip her shoulders with the intention of pulling her back to make her look at me and explain the intrusion. That's when I hear it. Loud wailing sobs pour from her in the most sorrowful sound I have ever heard. "Blue? What is it?"

I wrap my arms tightly around her, holding her close, forgetting all about the shower that drenches her hair and soaks her clothes.

"Talk to me, Blue." She tries, but her words are so garbled and all I can do is hold her, rocking us slowly side to side. I glance up and find both my parents standing in the bathroom doorway, brows furrowed with worry.

Abandoning my shower for much more pressing matters, I grab us towels, toss one around my waist, one around Blue, and lead her out to the living room to sit on the couch. My parents follow close behind, cooing to Blue, begging her to breathe, to talk to us.

Dad flees to the kitchen, rummaging in a panic to find something to fill the cup he grabs. I can hear him mumbling to himself. "Coffee? No...shit. Tea? That'll take too long. Shit. Shit."

"Baby, Blue, talk to me," I coo to her, oblivious to the pet name that slips out.

"It's not fair! It's not fair! They can't do this!" she wails before burying her face in my wet chest.

"Sweetheart, breathe. Tell us what's going on." Mom kneels at our feet, stroking Blue's knee, face twisted in anxious anguish. Blue is like family. She's always been around. Mom and Dad treat her like their daughter. I can see Blue's cries have both my parents bent out of shape.

"California. They're trying to move to California. It's not fair!"

After we get Blue calm enough to explain, we learn that her dad got a job offer in California for a voice acting gig in some major kids' movie. She says her dad has a house already, picked out her new school, and even has their house going on the market as soon as next week.

"What does your mom say about all this? Surely, she isn't as gung-ho about leaving!" Dad's working himself into agitation. He's always had a weakness for a woman crying.

"She says it'll be like a vacation! She can't wait for 'California life,' whatever the hell that means."

"But...what about us?" My voice is weak. It's the first I've said since all this came out. Life without Blue? California. How far away is California? Blue buries her face in my chest again. My parents exchange glances, some silent words passing between them. They go into the kitchen, heated whispering barely disguised.

"What the hell are they thinking? Uprooting her life like that!" Dad's whisper is more like a growl.

"Maybe there's more to it that Blue hasn't had the chance to find out yet. Maybe—"

"Maybe what? Maybe her dad is starstruck and hasn't thought how this effects everyone else!"

"Shh! Dear, come on, you know it isn't like that. We've all been good friends for so long, surely there's something we can do." Mom's rational calm soothes me. Yeah, maybe there is something we can do.

"Like what? Talk them out of it?"

"I don't know. But we have to do something. Did you see the way Black looked at us? I've never seen that look in his eyes. They can't be separated like this. Not after all this time."

"Maybe...maybe I can come too." I nudge Blue, urging her to look at me. I don't know what look my mom is whispering about, but I know my heart feels like it's on fire, my stomach churning in a cold knot.

"For fuck's sake, they might only be fourteen, but they've been in each other's lives since they were learning to talk!" Dad storms from the kitchen. Mom comes back to us, but the sound of the front door flying open has us all holding our breath. Mom mouths at me to stay here before running out after him.

"Dad says I can visit anytime I want. 'I'll make enough to fly you back every weekend, it won't be so bad, you'll love it, you'll see!'" Blue makes fun of her father, making a face at his lies. I might still be a kid, but even I know all that flying back and forth wouldn't be possible. "Besides, you saw how upset your parents got. They aren't gonna let you move too."

She's right. Of course she's right. But there has to be some kind of solution.

"I'm not going back. I'm never going back there. Don't let them take me!" Blue wails, her tears soaking my chest.

"Then let's run away together. You can't move to California if they can't find you!"

"You mean it?" She sits up, excitement replacing the despair in her dark green eyes. "But where do we go?"

"I know the perfect place."

My parents eventually come back saying nothing more about it. Blue stays the night. Dinner is quiet with the dark cloud of California hanging over us. They think I'm losing my best friend. They think they're losing their daughter. But tonight, Blue and I will fix everything.

We paddled and camped here a few times last summer. The blow-up raft has only one small hole that patches easily. The batteries in the flashlights and the raft air pump are all still working. We decide to make do with the one sleeping bag I have, too afraid to risk sneaking over to Blue's house to find hers.

We've never tried to cross the river at night, but this is the only way we can stay together. We remembered the tent, bug spray, snacks, and bottled water. But it wasn't until our little raft banked on the tiny island land mass in the middle of the river that we realized we'd forgotten clothes. But it doesn't matter. We're free. We have each other, and that's all we'll ever need.

I THINK BACK ON OUR little adventure whenever life throws me a curveball. Even if it didn't turn out exactly like we planned, everything worked out in the end. It gives me hope that no matter what happens, everything else will work itself out just like back then. Especially when I have Blue beside me.

Three years have flown by. Blue's dad did move to California to take that job. But Blue and her mom stayed behind. Every chance her mom gets, she stays with her dad in Cali, Blue staying with us. Just about every summer is spent like that. Blue thinks her mom will move out there once we go off to college.

"What are you smiling about?" Blue elbows me.

"How much we cried when we were found out after we ran away."

"We should do that again." She hiccups, passing another shared beer back to me. How many is that now?

"Run away?"

"No, goof. I meant go camping on that little island."

"I'm pretty sure it's not there anymore. If it is, it's just flooded and muddy."

"Well poo, then we should find somewhere else. I wanna camp again. That was fun."

"Mm-hm, you just wanna be all alone with me in the woods." I nudge her, then make a mental note to toy with that fantasy later tonight.

"I can do that here, too," she slurs. Before I can ask her what she means, she's kissing me. Our sloppy beer tongues groping the other's mouth. Her hands run over my chest, fingers grazing my nipples. And I'm trembling.

Blue pushes me so that I lie flat on my bedroom floor while she towers over me. My hands dance under her shirt, cupping over her bra. I have to keep my knees raised to hide the evidence of my secret desire for her. This is just a game. Playful drunken groping and nothing more.

"Gimme the beer." She gestures for the bottle just out of reach. I have to sit up to get it and take full advantage of her unsuspecting mouth in the process. What would she think if she found out how much I live for this game? I hand her the bottle and then it's over. She returns to the anime episode that was forgotten, and I'm left aching for her.

"D'you remember when we used to practice making out?" I slur. I didn't think we drank that much.

"We were so bad at it too." She giggles, sipping the last of the beer. "We kept bumping teeth."

I guess that's sort of how this drunken groping thing all started. Blue wanted to learn how to kiss when we were around thirteen. She was too nervous to do it sober and stole some nasty vodka from her parents' liquor cabinet. We gulped it, not knowing how much to drink. And then we were making out, learning how to nibble, how to avoid hitting our teeth together, and how to follow each other's lead.

Now, anytime we get even a little buzzed, we kiss and grope, reliving an old innocent game. I wish she didn't have to be drunk to want to kiss me. I wish she would want to kiss me for real, not for practice, not as part of some game.

"Hey, Black?" Blue's words are so soft I nearly miss them. I love our nicknames. I love most when she says mine. Our parents used to say no matter what we did, we'd always come home black and blue. And somehow, those became our names.

"Yes, Blue?" Both of us hate our real names. Before we were dubbed those colors, I used to go by Al short for Alfred, a family name. She used to go by Angel, short for Angelica. I actually like her real name, but I love calling her Blue because, after all, we're Black and Blue. Our names only work because we're together.

"I want to lose my virginity."

"Who doesn't?" I wouldn't be surprised to learn we're the only virgins left in our senior class.

"I want to lose my virginity," she says again, "and I want it to be with you."

"I—what?" But she doesn't say anything more. She pretends to be very interested in whatever show she'd put on. Did I hear her right?

"I want it to be with you." She says this like an afterthought, eyes glued to the screen.

She says that but I still remember those baths we used to take together. I remember showing off our first whiskers of body hair. I remember the day she started her period and how she cried and cried from embarrassment when we woke up covered in the evidence.

She's quiet, and I think maybe she's already forgotten her drunken proclamation. She turns suddenly, pushing me to the floor and draping her body on top of me. Her hand slides up my thigh. Shit.

"Blue, we're shitfaced." I remind her of the obvious, hoping one of us finds some semblance of sanity before this goes any further.

"I want it to be with someone I trust. Someone I care 'bout. That's you, Black." Her hot whisper tickles my ear and I squirm. But I can't ignore the slur to her words, the sluggish grind of her body on top of mine.

"Okay, okay." I swallow. "Not tonight. When we're sober."

"Promise?" She smiles against my neck.

"Promise."

3. Sex and Root Beer

Just like before, when the lines were crossed, it was as if nothing ever happened the next day. This time is no different. At school, she's beside me eating lunch, chatting away without any indication of remembered promises.

I thought about it. That first time, the subject of every virgin teenage boy's spank bank. I wondered what it would feel like with Blue under me, her lips on mine, her nails digging into my back. Never in all those fantasies did I believe any of it would become reality. So I think nothing of it when she comes over that night.

"Ugh, my headache didn't go away until last period. Yours?" Blue sidles up next to me on my bed as I browse endless options for a movie to watch.

"Still lingering." I sift through horror flicks, her favorite. "How about one of the Halloweens?"

"Lemme see." She wrestles the remote from my grasp. "I'm feeling an anime."

The thought doesn't cross my mind as she picks an anime and settles beneath the covers beside me. I forget about our drunken promise when her head settles on my chest. I doze from the remnants of our hangover, the result of too many beers too late on a Wednesday night. And I forget words like *virginity* and *promises*.

"Hey." I'm nudged awake, Blue's sharp elbow digging into my ribs. "We fell asleep. What time is it?"

"Nine? When the hell'd that happen?" I stare at the time on my phone in a half-asleep daze. At least the headache has finally faded.

"I'm gonna head home."

"It's late, just stay." I grab her and pull her to lie beside me.

"Can't. There're a few things I gotta do before tomorrow." She struggles in my grasp, but I squeeze tighter.

"What's tomorrow?" Is there a test I should be studying for that I've forgotten all about? A presentation maybe?

"Tomorrow's the big day. I want to be ready." She slithers from my embrace, sits up, and smiles some secret smile. "You promised, remember?"

And I'm wide awake.

"W-wait. Wait. That's happening? This is a thing?"

"It will be. Tomorrow night. Like you promised."

I sit up, massage my temples for some secret rewind button to replay the past, something to reveal the foggy details of last night. I didn't think that was serious. I didn't think she was coherent enough to make a promise like that, to *remember* a promise like that.

"Blue..."

"But tonight," she pulls my hands from my face, "I want a taste of what's to come."

I'm frozen beneath the cool touch of her hands on my cheeks. I'm petrified under the unfamiliar twinkle in her gaze. Her lips startle me. Her body moves over me, knees on either side of me, fingers lacing through my hair. A kiss that I'm still not sure is happening, deepens.

I melt. Promises forgotten. Pasts and baths and innocence disappear. There's a tangy strawberry candy hidden somewhere in that mouth of hers and I find myself desperate to find it. Our first sober kiss. She's kissing me. Because she wants to. Well, because of some promise I'm not entirely sure was real. But Blue's mouth is on mine, her tongue is caressing me, her teeth are nibbling my lips.

She pulls away, rushing for my bedroom door. I lunge for her. Is this really happening? Pinned between me and my door, Blue's wide eyes stare up at me. My thumb massages her lower lip. Was it all a beer-fueled dream? I lower my head to hers, brushing my lips softly over hers. She doesn't push me away, doesn't resist my kiss.

"Black." She coos. Her head tilts back, her lips parting, eyes sliding closed. I touch my upper lip to hers, easing into the kiss. Her hands fist in my hair, my mouth forced down on hers. And I'm grabbing her legs, wrapping them around my waist, pressing her harder into the door, and devouring her mouth.

"Mm, Blue..."

"Mmph." Her words are lost in the kiss.

Shit.

What the hell am I doing?

"Sorry. I'm sorry." I pull back, breathless. She drops from my waist, her face flaming.

Then she's gone. And I'm left reeling, aching for the fulfillment of that promise.

Are you sure about this? I text her about an hour later. My blood roars in my ears.

U promised. Is her only response. I want to ask her if she's all right. If I took things too far. What is she thinking after that?

But are you sure?

Yes & excited. Rnt U? She's excited? Okay, she's excited. She's excited!

Scared.

Me 2 but I trust U

She trusts me. No pressure.

I can still feel your lips. Night! She texts again. I stare at the words, the spelled out, unabbreviated words. What do I say to that? What *should* I say to that? She can still feel my lips. I can still feel her body pressed against mine. And my cock hasn't stopped throbbing since she left.

I type and delete and type and delete. *Was it too much? Are you okay? I can taste you too. I'm hard. Could you tell I was turned on when I was kissing you? Did you like it?* But nothing feels right. Or I'm too chicken. Or too confused at what role I'm supposed to be playing in all this. I have a lot of work to do.

WE WALK HOME TOGETHER after school. I'm going slow, forcing her to match my pace. I wanted to drag my feet, to give her time to really think it through.

"This is going to work," Blue proclaims. At first, I think she might be reassuring herself of my ability to perform, but then she says, "But we have to be completely honest with each other. About everything."

"Okay." I'm always honest with her. About everything. Almost everything.

"Things won't be weird, if that's what you're worried about."

"How can you be so sure?" Of course things will get weird. What if I don't live up to her expectations? What if she can never look me in the eyes again? Will this be the last night she'll feel safe with me?

"Because I trust you."

"What if that's not enough, Blue?"

"Black." Her hand grips my wrist. I'm pulled to a stop. Her lips devour me before I can react, and I find the protests lapped away by her tongue. "We don't have to. But that'll mean you broke your promise."

Her smile is so smug as she skips away from my embrace. She has me, and she knows it. I would never break a promise to her.

"HEY, BLUE!" MOM STIRS some kind of stew over the stove and glances over her thin shoulder when we walk in. "You staying for dinner? It's goulash."

"She's—"

"Yummy, sounds great! Yup, I'm staying the weekend!" Blue cuts me off, and I'm left standing abandoned in the kitchen as she continues skipping toward my bedroom.

"She's in a great mood today," Mom remarks.

For a moment, I contemplate sitting in the kitchen with Mom and submitting myself to her barrage of mom questions. School's great, we learned about sin, cosin, and tangent conversions in Trig 101 today. No, I don't have any girls I'm crushing on; oh, but there is one waiting in my room for me to take her virginity.

But I say nothing, am asked no questions, am given no buoy in the raging sea of whatever the hell is about to happen. She said she was staying the whole weekend. Why did I expect this to be a one-night stand kind of thing and then everything would just go back to normal? An entire weekend with something like this hanging over my head? Is Blue trying to give me plenty of time to make such a move?

I stand in awkward silence in the door of the fridge, staring at sodas and beers and various withering veggies. Mom browses an old cookbook and stirs, unaware of my silent pleading. The most important day of any teenage boy's life is on the horizon, and all I want is to run to my mother and make her tell me to wait until marriage or not to risk ruining my friendship with sex.

Sex. Blue wants me to have sex with her. She wants me to kiss her and touch her and slide inside her and...

"Long day, sweetie pie?" Mom asks, ditching the wooden spoon to drown in the red goo before pinning me beneath those probing, all-knowing eyes.

I grab two root beers, pop the top on one and sip through the foam. What can I tell her, what can I ask? Mom, how do I take a girl's virginity? How do you know when the time is right? Mom's graying auburn hair glistens under the sunbeams streaming in the kitchen window. For a moment, it's like she's my guardian angel sent to guide me through this. I want to appeal to those deep-brown eyes and search for the answers to questions I'm too terrified to voice. There's so much wisdom in the soft lines of her face. Little of her delicate features managed to be passed to me, and I find myself wondering if Blue would have liked if I had more of my mother's beauty and less of my father's sharp, aggressive attributes.

"You could say that." It's all I can manage to say. I silently pray she has a mom-moment and reads my mind for the truth.

"Is it about a girl?" She only asks this half-jokingly. My mom and dad and even Blue's parents joke about us staying single virgin best friends until we're old and gray and sharing a room at a nursing home.

"Actually, yeah." Her eyes widen with initial surprise before narrowing with this mischievous gaze, and I feel like maybe I should've just followed Blue to my room and faced this head-on.

"What's Blue have to say about it?" She knows something. The way she said it, the way she's looking at me, she suspects... Shit.

"Um...I think she's all for it. I mean, she supports it and..." I struggle over the words. What the hell can I say? It was Blue's idea. How can I get out of this conversation ASAP? What if Blue walks in on me groveling at my mom's feet to make it all better and tell me what to do? That wouldn't be very sexy.

Sexy. That's what I need to be for this to work. Can *I* be *sexy*?

4. Exploration

"Black!" Blue calls from my bedroom, and an image of her flashes before my eyes. Naked, sprawled on the blankets, impatient for the deed to be done. Mom shrugs, turning back to the goulash with a smug smile much like Blue's earlier on the sidewalk. She knows.

My heart beats an erratic tempo in my ears, faster and faster with each step nearing my bedroom. This is nothing but two best friends, who trust each other, who care for each other, sharing an important transition into adulthood. Nothing more, nothing less. A promise to be fulfilled, a bandage to be ripped off.

I'm taken aback by the sight of her fully dressed and settled into my bed like it's any other weekend. I slide in beside her, handing her the second root beer and thinking nothing of the dark TV screen. When she offers to set my root beer beside hers on my nightstand, I hand it over without question. It isn't until her cold hands slide around my neck and her bare leg stretches over my lap that my sluggish mind catches up.

"But—" Her black curls tangle in my fingers. Her strawberry-flavored lips and root beer tongue invade my senses. The rough denim of her skirt bunches between us. This is Blue. The girl I've known for so long, I don't even remember the first time

I met her. One day she was just there, living beside me, in class beside me, growing up beside me. She filled a Blue-shaped hole that I never remember being empty. And now she's on top of me, eating up my soul.

I thought I would have all weekend to work out a plan—and my nerve—before anything would happen. I thought it would be sometime deep in the night, when both of my parents would be sound asleep, and the only witnesses would be the crickets creaking beyond my window.

But Blue is kissing me. Fervent, passionate, desperate kisses. Here? Now? There's still so much I need to do, so much preparation not yet in place. Her hips begin this grinding gyration against me, and I cry out in surprise at how damn good it feels. Only then do I realize how painfully hard I already am.

"Shit. Blue—"

"Mm-mm." Her lips hum their protest against mine. My head swims.

"Dinner soon." My reminder seems to have the opposite effect. Her hips pump faster, her tongue laps with increasing fervor. "Ah! Shit, they'll hear!" I hiss, pulling her hungry mouth away by fisting my hands lost deep in her mass of hair.

"Then be quiet." Blue smiles that smug smile. "Just a little fun. Give us both something to think about until tonight." Her voice pants out a strained whisper.

So this isn't it? She just wants to fool around a little until dinner? Okay, I can manage that. Just fooling around. That's easy. That's drunken playful handsy fun. That's innocent enough. Her eyes betray her anxiety, and I wonder if she's afraid I'll back out. I read up all through the night, trying to be prepared, trying to be as experienced as a virgin can possibly be. Everything I read said she should be flushed on her cheeks and chest, that her eyes should be heavily lidded. That's how I'd know she was aroused. But I see nothing that indicates this is anything more to her than sharing a drink.

I pull her mouth back to mine, holding her head steady and setting a slower pace. This time I lead her. I guide her hips to a slower, steadier pace and stroke her tongue to follow mine. Her body relaxes into me, submitting to my lead.

Explore her mouth delicately, swirl tongues in a slow dance, allow her to get acquainted before trying any fancy moves.

I focus on everything I'd read, paying particular attention to any little sounds she might make to tell me if I do something she likes or doesn't. But so far, she's silent, following along without protest, without any of the gumption she had before I took over.

There's a moment's hesitation where I wonder if I should just stop while we're ahead and leave this until later, until we've had a chance to cool our heads and talk through what comes next. Blue jumps at my sudden slack, ripping her shirt over her head and diving her tongue back into my mouth with such force I nearly gag at the sudden haste. Her hands leave my neck where they'd steadily clung and fumble violently behind her back.

"Hey." I still her arms with hands to her elbows. Her brow is furrowed, and her eyes glazed with the task of forcing this to happen. "Blue, baby, relax. It's me. It's just me."

Her eyes clear, her shoulders sag with the reassurance I offer in my voice. If I'd had any time to think about all of this, really think about it all, my saner mind might wonder why her virginity was suddenly such a burden she must purge immediately. I might ponder the ferocity with which she tries to throw such an honor on me.

But those thoughts will have to be mulled over later. Now the only thoughts in my head are the next steps to the little move I mapped out. The culmination of all that I'd read, tips and tricks and secret maneuvers, all with the intent to make music from her throat. I want to hear her, hear that she wants this as badly as she's trying to convince me.

I've seen her shirtless, swapping her shirts for mine to sleep in. The frequent glimpses of her bras did not prepare me for the black lacy bra that she wears. One I've never seen, one that highlights and draws the eye to all the right places. My cock flexes beneath her and her eyes widen when she feels it. Fearful of her reaction, I freeze, only to notice a blush spread across her cheeks.

Encouraged by the sight, I pull her arms from behind her back and urge her to dig those slender fingers into my hair. I kiss her gently to soothe her frantic worry. Without my guidance, she moves her hips in synch with our slow kiss. I trail my fingertips up her side, working my way to her spine, higher, higher.

She moans. I'd heard moans before. Movies, anime, porn. But the sound she makes sends a shock though my entire body. I fidget with the clasp, attempting all the tricks from the numerous videos I'd watched. The twist maneuvers, the "pretend it's a soda can, pop the top" method. But the clasp remains steadfast. Thankfully, all the suggestions had one major pointer—distract. While one hand coaxes the tight clasp to surrender, I trace the cup of lace with the other hand, caressing the swell of her breast and working my way to her shoulder. Easing one bra strap down her arm rewards me with another moan.

"Blue..." My own moan betrays me, revealing how far I've strayed beyond performing a task at her request. I feel the heat of her grinding against my denim-covered cock and want so damn much to skip dinner. Desperate to feel more of her, I abandon the distraction technique and tackle that clasp two-handed. It relents with ease and suddenly, it slithers from her, exposing such perfect and plump breasts that knock soul from body, breath from lung.

She looks embarrassed at the exposure, but I notice she stops from covering herself, returning her hands to my hair. She presses those bare beauties against my chest and another moan escapes me. I ease her feverish body away, running fingertips up her flat stomach, the small portion that isn't covered by the bunched denim of her skirt. She jumps at the graze of one finger along the underside of her breast.

This is nothing like our drunken groping of the playful past. The fullness of her breast overfills my hand, and all I can think is how I've managed to miss such an opportunity for this long. Her skin is so smooth and warm, her heat boiling me from the inside.

I want her. Fuck, I want her so badly. Would I be betraying her for wanting this as desperately as I do? Is there some fine print in our promise I'm violating with my burning desire for her? Focus on the next step. Focus only on that.

I have to time this just right. I've thought it, acted it out in the dark of last night, planned it so perfectly I even dreamed it. Steeling myself against the nerves thrumming through the desire, I launch my little attack. One hand pulls her mouth tight to mine, one hand shifts over her breast at the ready.

Just as I knead her nipple between thumb and forefinger, I run the tip of my tongue along the roof of her mouth. Something strange happens. Her body trembles, her hips push hard into me. She pulls her mouth free from me, throws her head back, and gasps in such rapid succession I can't tell if I've done something good or very, very bad.

Blue collapses over me, head to my shoulder, arms limp beside us, breaths teasing my neck.

"D-did you just—?"

"I think so...it happened so fast." Her whisper is weak, her voice fading into the quiet of our hushed labored breaths.

Liquid escapes me, little beads of burning anticipation at the realization of her orgasm. I did it. The rarest achievement during her first time and I've done it without even trying. My little attack was aimed at nothing more than to ease my name from her throat. Instead, Blue came on top of me. She came because of me. She came against my throbbing, aching cock.

I can't stop the ill-timed groan before it rumbles from my chest. Her hips jerk the smallest amount and I find myself gripping her hips, making her grind harder, faster. I'm so sensitive. I can feel it. I'm close. Her hands grip my shoulders, her head falls back, and her back arches, pushing her breasts to my face. As she grinds away my sanity, I lean forward, capturing a puckered nipple between my lips. Fingers twist in my hair, holding me to her.

"Black..." She says it.

And I convulse beneath her, saturating my boxers, plastering the thin cotton to my thighs, drenching the denim between us. I stifle my cries into her sweat-slicked breasts.

She chugs her root beer, panting between gulps. She sprawls on the bed beside me. All I can do is remain frozen as I attempt and fail to reconnect my brain to my body.

"If it's going to be anything like that..." But she doesn't finish the thought. My disconnected brain doesn't register her words. She offers me her root beer and I finish it, despite my own sitting barely touched on the table within reach.

"I should, uh, get cleaned up." I rise to find unsoiled clothes but am stopped with her hand on my arm.

"Wait. Could I...would it be okay if... Can I see it?"

Puzzled, dazed, I stare at her. Instead of waiting for my response, her hands work the clasp of my belt. Confused, I lean back and allow her to unfasten my belt and pants. When she succeeds, she merely sits back, waiting for me to do something.

"Pull them down," she whispers, eyes glued to the dark wet circle on my jeans. Vibrating and floating, I obey on autopilot. Rising and falling into coherent thought, I ponder the strangeness of her curiosity. When I'd thought she wanted to see the now limp part of me that she'd only moments ago been grinding against, she surprises me by swirling her finger in the thick white clinging to my thigh. I tremble from her touch.

Between her fingers she stretches the white substance, watching as it snaps apart. Then, to my embarrassment, she sticks her fingers between her lips, suckling her fingers clean.

"Hmm. They said it was going to be salty but it's sweet. I like it," she says matter-of-factly.

I fell asleep. And had a graphic and intense sexy dream starring my innocent Blue. And exploded into my jeans. That's all it was. Those perfect taut breasts couldn't possibly have filled my hands. That firm little dark pink nipple couldn't have been suckled between *my* teeth. Her moans most certainly weren't mixed with the sound of *my* name.

5. A Black Cat's Kiss

Blue elbows me.

"Huh?"

"Jeez, son, your mother wasn't kidding. You really do have your head filled up with some girl, don'tcha?" Dad chuckles, Mom elbows him harder than Blue nudged me.

My face flames. I scoop goulash into a bowl and scurry to my room, Blue close behind me. I don't taste it. I barely register the too-hot stew until it has seared my tongue. The tongue that tasted Blue's strawberry mouth.

"Was it okay?" Blue's words swirl through the vacant thoughts in my head.

I turn to her, staring blankly. What would she care if Mom's goulash tastes all right? No, she's talking about earlier. The dream. She's asking if she was good in my dream. Very good, I imagine telling her.

"Yeah," I say simply.

"Is it weird?" The worry in her eyes, the sad lilt of her voice, the untouched food she swirls on her spoon, hit me.

"I didn't think it would be like *that*." She said we need to be honest for this to work. I will be transparent. I don't disguise the dreaming wonder in my voice and relax when I see the worry leave her eyes.

"Me neither." Her head nuzzles my arm and she settles there, leaning on me as she devours her food with newly discovered hunger.

I can do this. If tonight is anything like earlier, I won't need to worry about living up to her expectation and fulfilling this promise. That all-consuming desire takes over and all fretting thoughts fade away.

The rest of the night eases into that comfortable pace we share. None of the awkwardness I feared may surface becomes reality. Nothing about the heat of her body pressed beside mine conjures any anxiety at tonight's agenda. But I find myself yearning to pull her closer at the romantic bits of the anime she watches.

I decide against holding back. The only way to maintain this heady haze of what just happened and what's to come is to fully embrace the new role she's asked me to play. She doesn't object to the arm I drape around her or to the probing of my fingers to lace through hers.

I want to kiss her. A no-strings-attached, simple, beautiful kiss. But I have to think about this. She asked me to take her virginity. Does the intimacy of a kiss belong outside of such agreements? If I lean over, press my hungry lips to her succulent pair, would she take this as an invitation that it's beginning?

"Can I kiss you? Just a little?" I blurt the words, brain floating off somewhere in the ether, abandoning my mouth to impulse. Blue nods. I gingerly cup her chin, pulling her face to mine. Her eyes are squeezed tightly shut. Her teeth nibble her lower lip.

"Baby Blue," I whisper. My words startle her. Dark green eyes pop open, her jaw drops ever so slightly. That's when I kiss her. Gentle, slow, delicate. Her hands fist in the front of my shirt. The ending credits of the forgotten episode blare, startling us apart. I chuckle awkwardly and stifle the urge to apologize.

"I think I'm ready," she says in soft declaration, turning off the TV and tossing the remote to the floor. The sudden arrival of my performance terrifies me. I can't do this. There's no way I can do this.

"Okay." My impulsive mouth decides for me. It's too early. A meager eight on the dot. My parents are likely curled up together on the sofa in the living room, unaware at the milestone about to be reached down the hall.

I pull her to lie flat on the bed and tower over her, staring into the silence of her gaze. Her trembling fingers tug at the hem of my shirt, urging its unceremonious removal and I oblige. I remain towering over her, making no other move in this dance. It's best to let her set the pace, let her acclimate to her own endeavor. Pointed tips of her fingernails trace the lines of my torso. The sharp edge of freshly filed points prickle my flesh under her touch. The sudden image of Blue as a black cat strikes me. Her thick black hair, her deep green eyes, her tight lithe body, her new sharp claws.

Tonight, this black cat is mine.

Blue suddenly sits up, forcing me back to prevent the collision of our heads. She fights her own shirt, struggling to pull it over her head. I stop her, a gentle touch of my rough hand to her delicate wrist.

"We have all the time in the world." I lie on my side, face her, and urge her to mirror me. When she slides into place, I tuck a stray curl behind her ear. "I want to take my time with you tonight."

"Sorry. I'm just nervous." She stares at my chest when she says this, a blush of a different kind stealing over her cheeks.

"Me too. So let's take this slow. Okay?"

My plan was to prepare myself when I brushed my teeth for bed. I wanted to be drained before this, as ready as I could be to last as long as she needed. Instead, I'm going into this with the hot memory of her release on top of me, the echoes of her moaning my name sounding in my ears, the taste of her tart tongue on my lips. Slow is the only way to go.

I focus only on kissing her, stroking her back, and holding her close. I let her lead in our kiss and find it so much more passionate than my following-the-steps method. Our awkwardness fades with each passing minute spent exploring the other's mouth. Her hands explore over my chest, one fingernail grazes over my nipple.

"Ah!" The intensity of the touch and my reaction catch us off guard.

"Sorry!"

"More." I mumble into her mouth.

The soft pinch of her fingers over my nipple has me trembling. I bite her lower lip by accident. She yelps but the sound turns into something almost like a moan. I try again, lighter this time, and slip my hand under the front of her shirt.

"Black, please." Her breathy plea gives me pause. Please stop? Please give her more? "Help me take it off."

She twists to straddle me, and I pull the shirt off her. I bend to her chest, whispering soft kisses on the swells of her breasts. When I dip the tip of my tongue into the tight shadows of the black lace, she arches over me, my cock throbbing at the onslaught.

"Too much," she declares, rolling to lie beside me. "Too many clothes. Take off your jeans." Blue wiggles out of her denim skirt. I hurry to free myself from my own constricting denim prison. She slides back over me, my cock prodding her with its persistence. I see doubt flit over her features as she sits atop me, thin fabric separating her heat from my hard shaft.

I twist to pin her body—and her doubt—under my weight. And I kiss her. Slow. Slower. Her resolve feels as though it's slipping now that we lie pressed so close together with minimal fabric between us.

"Are you sure about this? We don't have to." Her reluctance stirs my own insecurity. Her face twists and I fear she'll burst into tears.

"I couldn't tell earlier. Through your jeans. It's bigger than I thought." She pulls me close, burying her face into my neck. "I'm scared. It's gonna hurt."

"Blue, baby." Her breath hitches. I ease from her grasp and meet her gaze. "We don't have to. If you still want to try, I'll go slow. And be as gentle as you need. If it hurts too much, we can stop. We can always stop."

"Okay. I want to. I really want to. Yeah, okay. I trust you, Black." Her hands frame my face. Her shaking, tiny hands.

"Besides," I nip at her lips, "that's later. Much later."

She towers over me with renewed vigor. Her eyes never leave mine as she unhooks her bra and slides the black lace down slowly, slowly. Little by little flushed pink flesh is revealed to me. Blue tosses the bra to the floor before gripping my wrists and bringing my hands to cup her breasts. At the cool connection of my palms to her soft nipples, we arch from the pleasure, twin moans dancing in the silence surrounding us.

"Shh," Blue giggles, leaning over me. "It's so hard to stay quiet."

"I wish we didn't have to. God, I want to hear you."

"Me too."

I want to hear what my touch does to her. I want to hear her moans, hear my name in that sexy tone. I want to burn all of it deep into my mind to conjure later, on nights when I'll lie alone after this, aching for more of her.

Her mouth finds me, her strawberry tongue the only taste worthy in this world. Any other taste buds can dissolve if it means this taste of her can be heightened. My senses surge, overwhelmed by all of her. The scent of our mingling sweat, the hushed moans on her tart tongue, the slide of her body on top of mine.

"Oh, Baby Blue."

"I love when you call me that." Her lips ignite fire along my neck. But when her mouth closes around my nipple, I grip her hips to steady myself. I have never felt pleasure so sharp, so intense as it is now, her mouth hot, her tongue lapping, and without any movement in her hips. It is then that I notice the smooth flesh my fingers dig into, a small strip of fabric lines her hips and nothing more. A thong. Dear God, she's wearing a thong.

Feverish fingers trace the lace around her hips. The stray thumb of my hand wanders between us. I caress over the fabric, pressing the spot that makes her breath hitch. Her teeth trap my nipple, biting hard when I rotate my thumb.

"Black!" Her harsh whisper of my name shakes me to my core. Slow. Slower. "Now, please. Now. *Now*."

She rolls beside me, waiting for me to climb on top of her, to slide inside her, to make good on that drunken promise of just the other night. When I try to ease her into slow kisses, trail soft touches along her sides, she grows impatient. She jerks the lace from her hips, pulling the thong down her thighs. I pull the thin thing the rest of the way, gliding fingertips along her legs, and watching her intensely.

One minute we're wrapped up in this together, following the other's lead, taking control, teasing, pleasing. And the next, Blue is frantic to get to it, desperate to rid herself of the burden that is her virginity. I don't want her to relax. I want her to yearn for this. I want her to writhe with need for me.

I know what I have to do. Teeth graze her thrumming pulse. Hands scrub, rough and firm, over soft mounded flesh. Callused fingers knead her soft nipples into tight peaks. I grip her throat, holding her as my tongue dances lower. Will she taste of the strawberry candy? Will she be unable to smother her screams of pleasure?

I bite hard over her protruding hip bone just to hear her squeal. Her hands fist in my hair and her frantic whispers snake through the pounding in my ears.

"Black, wait. Not that. It's okay, you don't have to do that."

Her words give me pause. Is the taking of her virginity all that I am allowed? These kisses, the touches, her affection, nothing more than extensions of that sole agreement? Is the act of my tongue dipping to taste her beyond what she considers acceptable between best friends?

I test a theory by trailing wet kisses along the imprint left behind from the waistband of her thong. Her legs spread farther apart, her hips arching the slightest bit against my lips.

"Are you afraid, Blue?" I whisper, my hot breath aimed *there*. I glance up at her. Her arm is draped over her eyes, pressing firmly to block out the light. She lies beneath me, bare, beautiful, and vulnerable.

6. Promises Kept

"I trust you." But her words are weak.

I'll earn her trust. Focus on the sounds she makes. Let her voice guide my actions. Soft. Careful. Slow. I settle between her thighs, watching her for any signs of pulling away. I huff a warm breath over her, and she sucks in through tightly clenched teeth.

One gentle kiss over her. She jumps at the contact, biting her lip to stay silent. My lips slick with her, I lap at the taste. Unable to stop the groan before it escapes, I bury the sound in the softness of her inner thigh.

"You taste so good." The words will embarrass me for the rest of my days, I know. But I want to reassure her, soothe any worries that hide behind her trust. Her jaw clenches with the subtle slide of my tongue inside her. She's tangy, she's sweet. She's everything and more than I imagined.

She holds her breath when I thrust my tongue in and out of her. Her throat strains with choked whimpers at the twirl of my tongue over the hard nub I discover. Breaths hitch and pant, hitch and pant with every flick of that little nub.

"Mm…" My Blue, my baby, coos. She parts her thighs, arches her hips into my mouth, and plunges her fingers deep into my hair. I slide a finger into her, feeling the resistance of what she's so determined to destroy. "Black, please. *Please.*"

I can do this. I can take what she offers, and we'll go back to pretending a line was never crossed. I ignore the sadness that clenches my heart at that thought.

Her grip tightens in my hair, urging me above her. And she kisses me. No hesitation graces her lips. Her steady hands slip my boxers down. Blue whimpers, an apprehensive tension disguised in her desire. Movements no longer frantic, she guides me closer to her until the head of my cock presses against her. She trembles.

"Blue..." My voice is hoarse.

"I know." Her smile is sweet and sure. She holds me in place, waiting for me. "Ready."

Slow. Slower. I push into her. It's too mechanical, too disconnected. She's frozen in wait. Kissing her pushes me deeper, little by little. But too soon I feel the resistance within her. Sweat breaks out on my brow.

"I have to—"

"It's okay." Blue surprises me with the sincerity in her eyes. Her hands frame my face and she gazes into me, pleading with me not to look away. *I'm sorry, Blue.* She tries to hide the pain blooming across her face as I push through the barrier.

"Blue, baby, it's over. I'm all the way." I won't move until I'm sure the pain has eased. I couldn't yet move if she wanted me to. She's so slick, so much tighter than I could have prepared for.

I kiss to distract us both, her from the pain, myself from the clenching around me. But her stiff body loosens under me. And her whimpers turn to moans. Soon, her hips move against me, and my promise to hold on for her is threatened.

"Wait." I peer down at her, thrilled to find her chest flushed, her lips parted with excited breath. "Slow. I have to—slow. To hold on. For you."

"It feels so good." And her tongue twirls with mine, her hips pump far too fast.

"Fuck. Blue—"

"Please." Her nails dig into my back. I move. In, out. Too close, too soon.

"Oh, how I fantasized about this. Just like this. Just like this..." I'm babbling in my desperation to hold on.

"M-me too."

"Yeah?" I search her eyes for truth. She nods, nibbling her lip. Was it me in her fantasy? Is this everything she imagined? God, am I doing this right? Am I hurting her?

"Black." Her head tips back on her moan of my name. I freeze, dangerously close.

"I'm close." I ground out the words at her worried look. My body trembles, begging for sweet release.

"Touch me," her husky voice commands. She guides my hand to cup her breast, her body arching into me at the caress of my fingers on her nipple. Blue's hands frame my face, locking my gaze to hers. I feel bared to her, vulnerable beneath her penetrating green stare.

"I'm going to—" Her mouth assaults me, biting and suckling at my lips. "Coming! Black, I—" She just had to go and say my name.

"Ah, Blue! Me too." The sensations of her body quivering around me, the lustful glisten in her eyes, the sultry cry of my name, and I'm gasping at the powerful, almost painful waves coursing through me. My kiss captures the remnants of her moans.

Not ready for it to end, I caress her lips with my tongue. Still holding her gaze, I plunder in my search for the source of her taste. She holds me to her, enveloping my body in the slick heat of hers. For several minutes, we remain in this entangled embrace, my weight supported on my arms, my kisses slow, re-assuring. Careful not to hurt or jar her, I roll onto my back, keeping her close to my chest.

"Blue...are you okay?" I whisper into her hair. She nods. "Did I...was it all right?"

"Yeah. It was good, really good." Her smile calms my rising panic as she sits up. She eases me out of her, not disguising the pain from her features, then lies back on my chest. "Can we stay like this a little longer?"

"Of course, Baby Blue." Her curls wrap around my fingers as I stroke her head. I imagine each silken strand becoming a vining root, binding me to her, linking our bodies together as one.

"I think I'm making a mess on you. Something's coming out."

"Shh, I know. It's all right."

After a few short minutes, I gather her in my arms and slip across the hall into the bathroom, grateful to find the house silent and dark. Her glazed eyes sharpen, pinning me with a questioning look.

"You need to pee afterwards. It's really important," I inform her matter-of-factly. "Oh, and I set aside a few of my mom's pantyliners in case you need them." I pull the small stack from the back of the vanity drawer where I'd stashed them.

"You know a lot about this."

"I researched all of it last night. Everything I could think of. I wanted this to be done right for you."

"I got blood on you," she says, bashfully turning her face from me as she sits on the toilet. "I can't go with you watching."

Not ready to leave her side, I turn on the shower, adjusting the water hotter than my taste, the way she likes it. To give her time to finish, I pretend to fiddle with setting the temperature. Her hands tremble in mine as I help her into the shower.

"I'm okay. Really." But she won't look me in the eye. The darkest towels I find are a washed-out burgundy-turned-purple. These should be dark enough that blood won't leave a noticeable stain. For a moment, I think of waiting my turn for the shower. But then I think of the thoughts running through her mind and I know. She's crying.

I slip into the shower behind her. My fears are confirmed. Her arms surround her, her shoulders shake. She clutches a hand over her mouth to hide the sounds from me. Gingerly, I reach for her, easing her to turn into my embrace.

"I'm sorry. I don't know why I'm crying," she sobs.

"It's okay. It's normal to cry. Just let me hold you." We did it. We found that pleasure, our first time, together. I'll always love her for it. We rock in the hot spray of the shower. I find myself humming some nonsense tune.

"Thank you, Black. For everything. Your research, doing this for me. Thank you." Blue cries into my chest.

"No, Blue. Thank you. For trusting me with something so important. For giving me this. I'll cherish this day forever."

She pulls back only to rise on the tips of her toes. I hadn't expected it. Her lips slide against mine in such a sweet caress that I cling to her, holding onto her affections with every dwindling tingle dancing under my skin.

I help her wash and rinse her hair, stand frozen as I watch her wash the body I'd just made love to. And my heart aches as I watch the blood swirl at our feet. She lets me wrap the towel around her. We brush our teeth side by side in silence. I retrieve her thong from my tangled sheets, wait for her to stick on a liner, then carry her to my bedroom.

I'd thought she'd want to gather her clothes and curl up in the spare bedroom wanting a little space. Or perhaps sleep on my floor wanting to be near. But instead, she snuggles into the blankets on my bed and waits for me to join her. She wears my discarded shirt from earlier, that little lined thong, and nothing more.

I contemplate stepping out of the room to discard my towel and slip on a pair of boxers but decide against it after reminding myself of the intimacy we've already shared. After quickly changing, I slip under the blankets beside her. She scoots close, pressing her body into me, and I wrap my arms around her.

"Are you tired?" Blue's whisper tickles my chest.

I'm wide awake, mind frantically replaying every moment, scanning for missteps, and searching for clues that could indicate her level of satisfaction with my performance. Sleep will no doubt evade me tonight.

"Not even a little."

"Can we talk for a while?" This isn't like her. If she wanted to talk about anything, she wouldn't hesitate, just launch right into it.

"What's on your mind?" My heart thunders in my chest. Can she feel it against her cheek?

"Did you like it? I—I mean, was I good—was it good?"

What the hell can a guy say to that? What if it was terrible for her and that's why she's asking? What kind of jerk would that make me if I sang the praises clutching to my tongue? Was she good! She could think it was terrible for me, it meant nothing to me. Or worse, she could find out the truth, how it meant everything to me.

"I—I don't know what to say." Shit. Even that was the wrong thing to say. Her head sags against my chest. "I don't want to say that it was incredible for me...if it was awful and painful for you."

"It wasn't, Black. I thought it was incredible. That you were." She sits up to peer down at me, her dark eyes glinting in the faint light. Her cheek is hot beneath my fingers. I wish I could kiss her.

"Was it like you imagined?" Was it everything she ever dreamed? Was it anything close to fantasy? Shit, should I have lit the room with candles? And music. There should've been music.

"And more." Her head settles on my shoulder. I pull her close, heart clenched at her words. "Was it weird? Being like that...with me?"

"No, not even a little. Was it for you?" But of course, I knew it wouldn't be weird to make love to her, considering how it's all I've yearned for. She shakes her head and I wonder how to keep talking, afraid morning will bring too much normalcy.

"Black?" Her voice trembles with my name. Fear spikes in my blood.

"Yeah?"

"Can I kiss you?"

Yes. God, yes, Blue. Kiss me until my lips bleed. My noise of affirmation is a strange grunt of tightly bundled nerves. I just took her virginity. Why the hell does the offer of her kiss suddenly make me shake with anxiety? She's leaning on her elbow, her mouth mere inches from mine. This is different. No. No, it isn't. I read about this too. The feelings of love that might occur for a short time afterward.

Featherlight whispers of her lips dance over mine. And I'm vibrating with newfound anticipation. She presses her lips down. Once. Twice. Little smack noises pop between us. And then her hands frame my face, her lips toying with me, tickling then pulling back, again and again.

"Blue." Fuck. It slipped out. A whimper, maybe a moan. Shit.

"Sorry." She pulls away, her apology sounding embarrassed.

"Don't stop." I grip her shoulders, urging that mouth close to mine. But I don't kiss her. I wait beneath her, starving for her touch.

When those lips finally descend upon mine, my breathing stops. I'd expected her to become frantic as she had whenever she took control earlier. But this is something else entirely. There's something sensual about her now, something delicate and beautiful. If it were possible to make love in only a kiss, Blue's kiss is as close as I could imagine.

Too soon, she settles beside me, falling quickly into a deep sleep.

What the hell was that about?

7. A Game of Questions

Restless by morning, I rise to make her pancakes. With chocolate chips. Piled high with whipped cream. I try to act normal, settle into a routine weekend of junk food, anime bingeing, and lazing in pajamas. But there's so much I want to ask. Was last night everything she'd hoped for? Is it something we can talk about?

"You're staring," she says with a smirk. She lies on her stomach at the foot of my bed watching anime. I can't help but wonder if I were to slip under the covers to lie beside her, if I'd catch a glimpse of that black lace thong peeking out from under her shirt.

"Sorry." I want to pull her close, to soothe her. Does she need comfort? Does she need the care of a lover or the support of a best friend? "How are you feeling?"

"I'm okay, Black. Really." Her small smile is reassuring, but I still feel unsettled. "Wanna go for a walk?"

"Yeah, sure." A walk to clear my head. A change of scenery away from that bed and the images that fill my mind at the sight of it.

"Pick me out something to wear, would ya?"

Over the years, we've accumulated bits and pieces of each other's clothing and have taken to keeping a small wardrobe at both our houses. Her stash of clothing in my dresser include numerous shirts, undergarments, another denim skirt, plain black shorts, and a tight pair of jeans. I toss the jeans, a bra and panty set, and a Metallica t-shirt her way.

After picking out my own clothes for the day—jeans and a plain black shirt—I strip without thinking only to stop halfway from removing the shirt I'd slipped on to make her breakfast. When I risked a glance at her, she was pulling up her own shirt. We freeze, shirts bunched under our chins, her bare breasts in full view.

She shrugs. Frozen, I stand awkwardly with my shirt half raised as she pulls off her shirt, slips on the bra, and tugs the clean shirt in place. It was all so normal. When she stays the night and asks me to pick out an outfit for her, she dresses in front of me all the time. But she normally sleeps in a bra. And I normally have enough sense not to stare.

"Sorry," I mumble, leaving the room for her to finish dressing without my probing stare.

We walk aimlessly, silently. My hands clench, unclench. Palms sweat. What the hell do I say?

"Black," Blue slips her hand in mine, "relax. It's just me." Her words mimic mine from last night. And I'm thinking about last night again. Dammit.

"I—I'm just worried. Are you okay? Does it hurt? Are you still bleeding—" I stop, and she turns to face me, her smile falling. "No, I shouldn't ask that. But I can't help wondering. Was it too much? Not enough? What do we talk about? *Can* we talk about it? Is that okay? Are you—"

"Hey, Black. Stop. Look at me." Her tiny hands grip my arms. She shakes me, staring up at me, pleading with me. "Yes, we can talk about it. You can ask anything you want. It's me, Black. It aches a little but there's no more blood. And last night...it was perfect. Everything was perfect."

Blue hugs me. I relax into her arms, fighting the peculiar urge to cry. She leads me to the elementary school where we always go to swing when we're bored.

"Remember when we used to play train?" Blue looks wistfully at the metal slide in the middle of the playground. I don't remember too much about elementary school, a few random embarrassing moments like crying in the middle of a presentation, pissing myself in first grade. But I remember Blue. I remember taking turns on the slide until we got too impatient and started riding down together. Soon we had a whole group we'd link up with and go down all at once.

"I was always the engine, in front. You were the caboose bringing up the rear of our group," I reminisce. We kick our legs in sync, swinging higher and higher.

"Yeah, until that new kid made fun of me once and so you made me sit right behind you every time after that." She giggles.

"I called you the captain's quarters."

"Quite a promotion for the caboose." Her smile looks so carefree. The black curly mass of her hair covers her face, flies wildly behind her, and twists around the chains. "First one's the engine!"

She's flying through the air off her swing and running the second her feet hit the ground. I clamber close behind. The simultaneous smack of our hands grabbing the ladder rail bar echoes in the calm afternoon. I scramble up the slide ladder after her. It's so much shorter and narrower than I remember. She has to raise her legs on bent knees to make room for me to awkwardly tuck my legs on either side of her. Before we're fully settled, she pushes off and we ease lamely down the hot metal.

"Well, that wasn't as fun as it used to be. I think you got fat." She chuckles, sitting at the bottom and making no move to untangle from me.

"Yeah right! I think your thighs got too thick!"

Blue flails back, forcing me to lie on the searing-hot surface. And we lie there, staring at the clouds, awkwardly wrapped at the legs, her head on my stomach.

"Do you ever miss it?" For a split second, I think she means our lame game of train. But then she says, "Being a kid, I mean."

"I guess I've never really thought about it. Not too much has changed since then." I immediately regret the words, forgetting last night for a mere second. Things have changed a lot. At least for me. And long before she moaned my name in ecstasy.

"Except for my big thighs, you mean." Her head twists up to flash a brilliant smile at me.

"Well when you put it like that, maybe I do miss how little they used to be," I pester back.

"Oh really?" She somehow manages to untangle our legs as she twists to half lie over me. "You had no complaints last night."

The playful ease of our banter disappears. Her head falls to my chest, my fingers digging into her hair of their own volition.

"Are you really okay, Blue?" I don't know what it is that I can't shake, why I have to keep asking her.

"Will you stop worrying?" She nuzzles into my massaging fingers. "Are *you* okay? Are *we* okay?"

She turns to look up at me. I don't know what to say. I'm not okay at all. I don't know how to answer if we're okay.

"I can't stop thinking about it. I don't want to make anything weird, I just want to be honest, like you said we should." My heart pounds and I know she can hear it.

"It's all I can think about, too. But that's normal, isn't it? It was a big moment, losing our virginity. If it happened with other people, don't you think we'd be asking each other a thousand questions?"

Of course. She's right. If she had lost it to anybody else, I'd want to know if she really consented. That he was careful and courteous. Did she regret it? Is she dating him now? Was he good in bed, a good kisser? I might even have been brave enough to ask if he was able to get her off.

"Yeah, I guess so. I hadn't thought about that."

"How 'bout we pretend it was with other people? And ask anything we want?"

I don't like the idea of pretending what happened between us, didn't. But I understand why she suggested it. It gives us both the freedom to ask without fear or shame. The rest of the day becomes this giddy game of asking questions back and forth, playing with this new idea she's come up with.

"Was he a good kisser?" I ask her on our walk back.

"Oh, the best." She smiles, hand innocently laced with mine. And I loosen into the game.

Lounging on floaties in the hot sun in her pool, she asks me, "Was she a screamer?"

"I don't know. My parents were home, so we had to be super quiet."

"Bummer. Maybe you'll find out next time, if you get to be alone with her."

"Maybe." I slide off into the cool water, the pounding in my ears dissolving under the heavy distortion of the water.

"What did she taste like?" Blue asks while the evening sun bakes our skin.

"Strawberries." I stretch on the soft towel. She reaches over and smacks my arm. "Seriously."

"No shit? Strawberries, huh?"

"Yup. What did he taste like?"

"Root beer." It's my turn to swat at her. She giggles, rolling onto her stomach to dodge my hand. I give her a look. "Oh, *that's* what you mean. Well...it was different. I don't know. Sweet, not salty. I can't think of anything to compare it to."

We have a picnic with sandwiches at the edge of a river not far from our houses. The game continues.

"How big was he?" I smile when she chokes.

"A little too big, honestly. I thought he was gonna tear me in half." But at my terrified look she adds quickly, "But it turned out to be perfect. And no, before you ask, it didn't hurt too bad."

"Did you wear any lingerie for him?"

"Sorta. I bought a sexy black lace bra and thong set for him."

My throat dries. So that's why I'd never seen it before. She bought it specifically for last night. She really bought it for me.

"Did he go crazy when he saw it?" My question is strained, and I can only hope she doesn't guess at the reason.

"He didn't say anything. But I think so. I hope so." Blue leans back on her elbows on the little blanket, her face tipped to the sky. She twists the question back on me. "Did she wear anything sexy for you?"

"Yeah," I cough. "Um, it was really sexy. I was speechless." I knew I'd forgotten something. An important step completely skipped. I fucked up and forgot to tell her how beautiful she looked. Her cheeks flush bright pink, and I think maybe I managed to make up for it a little.

She's so enamored with our little game that she curls up in my bed later that night. Maybe she'll sleep in my bed from now on. I can't help but hope.

"Was it her first time too?"

"Yeah, I had to be very careful not to hurt her. I'm still worried I wasn't careful enough. Was it his first time?"

"It was but it wasn't anything like I'd heard it would be. Every girl I know says the guys just go crazy for a few seconds and then it's over. But it was different. He took his time with me, really took his time. It was like he wanted to make sure I enjoyed it more than he did."

Even in the dark of my bedroom, I can see her eyes sparkling with the sincerity of her words. We're curled up facing each other, hiding under the covers like two kids up past their bedtime.

"Did you...? Did he manage to, y'know..." Her head cocks in confusion at my struggle to find the words. "Make you come," I mumble.

"Yeah, three times. The first time was when we were fooling around. And the second time was just a little bit right when his cock touched me. But I don't think he noticed. And then we came together." Her voice sounds husky.

"You came three times," I echo. My palms sweat. My heart hasn't stopped pounding since we started this game. And my cock throbs painfully.

"Were you able to get her off? How did you do it?" Blue scoots closer. God, I want to pull her against me, show her what this game is doing to me.

"I was trying to hold on, but she kept pumping her hips so fast. I had to get her there quick before I lost it. When I held her hips up in a certain way, I noticed her breathing changed. And when I pounded harder into her, it just happened. She moaned my name and I couldn't hold back anymore." I realize I'm panting. I have to get out of here. It's starting to hurt with every passing, throbbing second.

"Black." She whispers my name. Blue presses against me and before I can think to hide my erection, she's kissing me. Soft nips on my burning lips.

"Blue." I moan. She becomes frantic. There's a flailing beneath the blankets and then she's straddling me, fighting my boxers down before she plunges me into her.

"Fuck, yes, Black!" Her body writhes. Fuck, she's coming already.

I grab at her mouth and eat those words, those too-loud, too-hot words. Her hips are hard and fast, hard and fast. I sit up to hold her closer, to force her hips farther, to thrust deeper. She's having sex with me. I'm having sex with Blue. Not taking her virginity because we're two best friends who trust each other. Not drunken handsy play that goes too far. She's on top of me. I'm deep inside of her. And she wants it. Just because.

"Blue, baby. Fuck, careful, I'm so fucking close." I grind my teeth, but she doesn't let up.

"Come for me. Come." Her hot whisper in my ear, her sharp teeth on my lobe, and I'm lost.

"Oh, baby." The words tumble from my lips as she steals my release.

"I'm coming, too, Black." Her words get lost between my lips. Our breathing slows but she keeps kissing me. I ease back to look at her. Cheeks flushed, lips parted with her panting breaths, eyes heavily lidded. Fuck.

Her fevered flesh trembles at my touch, hands exploring more and more under her shirt.

"No bra," I gasp.

"I wanted to come to bed naked but wasn't brave enough." Her hands do their own exploration and I'm aching all over again at the pinch of those fingers on my nipples. She's found my most sensitive places already.

I want her under me. Before the thought solidifies, she's twisting us, pulling me on top of her. This time I can take it slow. This time I can take all night with her. I watch her carefully as I ease out of her then slide so painstakingly slowly back in. Those deep green eyes roll to the back of her head.

Many hours after we'd settled into bed to continue our game, we fall apart, gasping, spent. This has been the greatest weekend of my life.

"Is this okay?" Blue pants in the dark. "Is it okay if I want this again?"

"Are you asking if we can be fuck buddies, Baby Blue?" I chuckle. Is this okay. How could it not be? What fool would deny her such passions? What fool would deny himself such pleasure?

"Yes. I don't know. Can we?"

"I think my answer is obvious." I roll on top of her.

8. The Taste of Strawberries

My first night alone is restless. We spend many nights together, school nights and over weekends. But there are those rare nights we spend apart, enjoying the comforts of our own beds. I've always hated it.

I miss you, I text Blue a little after midnight, hoping she's at least able to find sleep.

What do you miss most? She responds almost immediately followed by a GIF of some cartoon character winking. Dare I hope she's restless for the same reasons? What do I miss most?

The taste of strawberries. I blush like a little kid as I wait for her response.

Not these? Her text is followed by a close-up picture of her perfect breasts.

Thanks for that. Now I'm hard.

Pics or it didn't happen, she challenges. I meet her challenge with a picture as requested, feeling giddy at the thought of her staring at that picture. Will she save it and look at it whenever she's alone and missing me?

I wait anxiously for her response. A minute passes. Then five. Then ten. The insecurity sets in. Should I have asked for a picture back? Did she only want a picture of my bulge under clothes? Is she waiting for more pictures? Did she fall asleep? The erection fades as I fight from calling her out of panic. All of this has me so out of sorts. I nearly cry from relief when my phone vibrates.

Oh, it's a video. It's dark and grainy but I can just make out the glistening folds beneath her fingers. I'm stroking myself to the video before I'm fully hard. Just before the clip ends, I hear a faint moan. My name. Oh God, she's moaning my name and touching herself.

I watch it over and over, edging close until liquid anticipation beads in my hand. I should reciprocate. Damn, I wish I could watch her video while recording my own. I come on video at the thought of her waiting in her room, fingers massaging in idle play, excited to see what I send back.

The video is shaky and just as hard to see as hers, but I'm grateful to note I cried her name without realizing it. Before I get self-conscious and chicken out, I hit send. Then spend the next several moments checking and rechecking that I didn't accidently send it to someone else. Twenty minutes pass. But I relax, thinking she enjoyed my video and fell right to sleep, fingers buried deep inside her. The vibration of my phone startles me from a light sleep.

I came twice, her text says simply. Fuck.

What the hell, Blue, I'm hard again!

Save it for me. I can't sleep the rest of the night. How am I supposed to get through classes tomorrow with all of this weekend floating around in my head? How the hell am I supposed to be close to her and not ache for her? Tomorrow, and for who the hell knows how long, I see a lot of awkward boners in my future.

She asked me to save this desire for her. Easier said than done. But it begs the question, when will I have her next? Maybe she's coming up with a plan. Maybe tomorrow I'll get attacked in some dark hallway at school. Or maybe we'll both claim food poisoning tomorrow night and play hooky together the next day.

By the time my alarm is set to go off in another hour, I've long since given up on sleep. And I failed to hold back from doing anything about this raging hard-on. I decide to get around for school lazily, brushing my teeth, then staring at my bedroom ceiling while I contemplate today's attire. I can hear my parents in the kitchen.

Does Blue like how I dress? Should I dress up a bit today? Maybe wear something that'll have her eyes glued to me all day? I smile at the thought but struggle to come up with any outfits that would achieve such a thing. The front door slams and I wonder which parent left early.

"Oh, good morning, you're up early, Blue. I think he's still asleep." I hear my dad's booming voice. Blue? Blue's here?

"I know, that's the point. I couldn't sleep so I decided I'd come over and wake him up!"

My heart's pounding in excitement. It's just Blue, here to wake me up. Why the hell does it feel like Christmas? She pushes my door open slowly, expecting me to be asleep. Her eyes widen when she realizes I'm staring back at her.

Without a word, she closes the door behind her, locking the handle with a flick of her fingers. I'm grabbing at her before she's halfway across the room and have to smother her squeal in a kiss as I flip her onto my bed.

The thought of my parents down the hall makes it hotter, naughtier. She makes quick work of ripping off her jeans and another new thong, this one a dark blue. Her nails scrape my thighs as she yanks my boxers out of the way. The moment I slip into her, she buries her face in my neck to stifle her moans.

"Fuck, already?" I whisper into her hair.

"I was up all night watching your little video, what did you expect?" she whispers, breathless, a sexy smirk on her tart lips.

"Me too, baby. I didn't sleep at all."

"Sorry."

"You can steal my sleep anytime you want." There's no more room for talk. Her hips are pumping, I'm thrusting, and the blaring of my forgotten alarm is background noise that goes unnoticed. But I try to hold on a little longer.

"Five more minutes," I tell her, holding her hips from their desperate pace. Five minutes pass in agonizingly, tantalizingly slow pleasure torture. The moment I hear both of them leave, seven minutes past my alarm as always, I slam into her.

"Sing for me, Blue, baby." I nearly choke on the words at the strain to last as long as I can. She is far from quiet, erupting in little tight screams of my name, moans that echo off my bedroom walls, and this sexy panting squeal when my hand slips under her bra.

I don't recognize the growling groans emanating from my own throat now that we're free to be as loud as we want. This need feels primal. My desire for her like some demon that's been chained in the basement of my psyche.

"No more nights apart. I can't handle it," Blue demands, nails raking down my back, head thrown back in ecstasy.

"Never again." It's naughty, it's risky, and a stronger man might have been able to resist. But I am not that man. And I capture her throat between my teeth, branding her for the world to see. She comes in a writhing, moaning convulsion that drags me with her. Her skin becomes slick under my lips.

"Did you give me a hickey?" She cups her neck where it is already blooming a wonderful rainbow of colors.

"Why yes, yes I did." My smile probably looks as demonic as it feels.

"Asshole." She smiles.

I'M IN A DAZE THROUGH all the morning classes. We sit close and vibrate with the closeness in the classes we share. By the time lunch rolls around, I've played her video mentally about a thousand times.

"We should go to the beach this weekend!" I announce the idea midway through some flavorless bite of a soy burger from the cafeteria. Blue followed me through every line, absently picking out all the same shit. Her food is about as neglected as mine. Our school friends surround us in their usual vibrancy. Allen, the loudest of the group, is the most excited about the idea.

"Fuck yeah! Babes in bikinis, yo!" he answers mid-chew, his lasagna spittle painting the cement at our feet. I'm grateful the school opened up this little outdoor courtyard for nice-weather lunches. Allen is a pain in the ass to sit across from on those narrow tables inside.

"Hey!" Tracie throws a tiny piece of a roll at Allen.

"I'm free this weekend." Colin nods, his free time normally taken up by some flavor-of-the-week chick from a town over.

Our school friends have always been a colorful bunch over the years. We find those outspoken but fun extroverts who love to talk over Blue and my usual quietness. It's like a game of people-watching we started in middle school. A misfit here, a jock there, sometimes a goth or two. A melting pot of friends we would surround ourselves with for the year.

It wasn't like we hung around them for the sake of mocking them when we were alone. It was nice to have the company. But after about a year, most of them would simply part ways. But other times, and more often than we care to think about, the friends we would spend all year with would push us away, uncomfortable with the closeness of our bond. Blue and I have never talked about it, just shrugged our shoulders and picked replacements.

"You're in a good mood, Black. It's not like you to wanna hang after school." Allen says all this with another full bite. Nausea swirls in my gut at the sight. Blue chokes off a giggle.

"What's so funny?" Tracie leans forward and pins a glare at Blue. There's always been a subtle level of animosity between the two that I've never been able to put my finger on.

"Yeah, what's going on, you two?" Colin interjects, pointing a pasta-coated fork at us. "Somebody's holding out a secret. You're both practically shaking with it."

"That's because..." Blue does begin shaking, wrapping her arms around her waist and struggling to hold back her fit of giggles. I'm sitting in the middle of all this, just as confused as the rest of them. "Black got laid over the weekend. I hear she had to stay home today to recover!"

A cold sweat coats me. Brat. She is so gonna it get when we get home.

"No fucking way, dude!" Allen claps me on the back.

"Well, that makes sense," Colin says with a no-nonsense nod. Tracie quietly picks at her food.

"Looks like Blue had a busy weekend too!" Allen proclaims, jabbing at her neck. The others lean over to stare. I can't help but smile at the blush spreading from her cheeks to her neck. Seems her little plot backfired. I cough over my own choked giggle. Her elbow meets my ribs and the giggles spill out.

"Well...look at that!" Blue stands, hands to her hips. "I guess I didn't have to recover at home today after all!" And with that, she saunters away, carrying their confused gazes with her.

Holy shit.

Holy shit.

One by one, it sinks in. Tracie gets it first, a soft but sharp inhale. Then Colin with a broad smile and elbow nudge. Allen is last, looking at me then at Blue's receding form in the lunch crowd. Finally, he claps me on the back again. I leap up to go after her and can't help but overhear their jeers.

"So, they finally fucked." Allen makes no attempt to lower his voice.

"Guess so."

"What the hell. Ew." Tracie sneers.

"Wanna tell me what that was about, Blue?" I finally catch up to her, pulling her to a stop.

"What? It's not like we're a secret...right?" The laughter fades from her eyes, worry replacing it.

"No, no of course not. Why do you think I wanted to do this?" I press a finger on her hickey. She smiles warmly and I forget we're in the middle of the cafeteria as I lean down to kiss her.

"Hey! Break it up!" A teacher points and yells from across the room. We break apart giggling.

"There, now everybody knows who I belong to," I proclaim proudly.

"As if that wasn't clear already." Blue's joke sounds a little forced. On the way to my next class and all through the rest of the day, I mull over my own words and wonder what I'd meant.

Who I belong to?

Now everybody knows...who I belong to...

Did I just make our fuck buddy relationship into something more? Is that even something she would want? The logical next step of a bona fide exclusive relationship between us seems daunting. I'm still wrapping my head around this most recent change. Dare I allow any hope to build at the possibility of Blue becoming mine? Truly mine?

9. All Pretend Mine

"It's already starting," Blue announces Friday after school while we wait for Colin to pick us up to go to the beach. It's only half an hour away to Lake Michigan, so we can get a few hours in before the sun sets. We were supposed to go this weekend but Blue and I pretended to have plans we'd forgotten about. Our feeble excuse was rejected with knowing chuckles and elbow nudges.

"What's already starting?" The sun is thankfully hot and the sky clear. I can't wait to ogle Blue in her bikini now that I don't have to pretend innocence.

"The rumors. People think we're dating."

"I'm sorry, Blue. I guess I was caught up. I forgot where we were when I kissed you." My excitement dies at the memory of my lunchroom mishap.

Blue shifts from foot to foot in my driveway. "Maybe...maybe they'll treat us different if they think we're a couple. Maybe people won't think we're so weird."

"I didn't think any of that bothered you." It's the first time she's ever said anything like that. No cars have passed on the street in some time. Where the hell is everybody?

"I don't know." She shrugs, her beach bag dancing on her shoulder. "It'd be nice to have some girlfriends. Y'know, to talk girl stuff with."

"You can always talk to me about anything, you know that." I wrap an arm around her and place a kiss on the top of her head. Her hair is tied in a lame bun at the nape of her neck. All I want to do is set her frizzy mane free.

"Yeah, right. Like you talk to me about everything like you would with dude friends. I don't recall you ever telling me about any of your wet dreams." She pouts.

"Is that what you think guys talk about?" Another shrug is my only answer. "I'll tell you about it next time I have one, then. But don't be surprised if it's about you." She squeals when I nuzzle the side of her neck.

"It better be!" Blue squirms from my hungry lips and burrows against me, her arm wrapping around my back. "You think...would you care if we played the part? Acted like a couple at school and, I don't know, held hands and made out sometimes?"

My heart hurts at her request. She really wants more friends. When did I ever delude myself into believing I was all she would ever need? How selfish can I be?

"I'm sorry I never realized how much that stuff bothered you. Of course we can, Blue."

"Yeah?" Hopeful green eyes pin me in place.

"Blue, baby, would you go out with me?" I didn't expect the painful excitement that burst through me with the utterance of those words. God, if only this were real.

"Yes!" She beams ear to ear, launching into my arms and smothering me in kisses.

"Guess this means I'll have to plan our first date, something you won't be able to stop talking about all the next day in school."

Colin flies into the driveway beside us in his mom's mini-van and the moment is ruined. I immediately regret this thoughtless suggestion that we hang out after school. All I want is to spend more time alone with Blue. It's all I've ever wanted.

Tracie barely speaks to any of us the whole time. Allen, oblivious, attempts to get her on his shoulders for a game of chicken. It isn't long until she returns to the blanket laid out on the sand to sulk, or tan, as she claims.

It's painfully obvious that we don't have much in common and have never been close, but despite myself, I find that I'm having more fun than I expected. At least, until the sun begins to set and we all settle on the blanket to dry in the last rays before packing up. With Blue nestled beside me, the scent of sand and water on her golden skin, thoughts of her earlier request return.

How long will my Baby Blue be mine? All mine, pretend mine?

"HOW'S THE FRIEND HUNT going?" I ask her as we loiter in the hallway for as long as we can until the minute bell rings.

"The what? Oh! Uh, not so well. I don't know. Maybe my weirdness has done its damage. I don't think any of the girls think of me as a girl." Blue says this but stands before me in pigtails and a pink dress. I don't think being seen as one of the girls is the problem.

"Maybe we're not obvious enough. I mean, I'm pretty sure we've held hands to and from school before. And not many people have seen us making out. You think we seem even weirder?"

"Whatever. If nobody wants to be friends with me, not much I can do about it." She shrugs, giving up so quickly.

Not ready to leave the fantasy of dating my Blue, I stay up all night, tossing and turning beside her, racking my brain for an idea. It hits me right at dawn.

"I'm gonna walk you to school but I'm playing hooky," I announce into her sleepy and adorable face. My blankets left an imprint on her right cheek and her pigtail-kinked hair stands in various directions. She is so damn cute.

"What? I wanna play hooky too! I don't wanna go alone!" she pouts. The thought of a full day of hooky with her has my cock tightening. Why haven't we done that yet?

"Just first period. There's something I gotta get. At lunch, don't wait for me, get your food and sit in our usual spot. When I get there, play along."

"Play along...what's going on? What are you up to?" She's rubbing her eyes, running fingers through her hair, yawning, stretching. And it is the most seductive thing I've ever seen.

"It's better if you don't know. But trust me, this way there won't be anybody who doesn't know we're a couple. You'll probably have all kinds of girls flocking to you after this wanting all the juicy details!"

Blue begrudgingly heads into school without me, and I make quick work of getting what I need. I don't let myself think about what comes next and how sad it feels that this is an act. I focus solely on the reason I'm doing this. For Blue. So she can get the friends she wants, or at least gain the attention of some classmates and hopefully turn them into friends.

I find her exactly where I'd asked her to wait and take a moment to stand there watching her. She's checking her phone, refreshing constantly, likely trying to see if I've messaged her. Her teeth peek out of her plump lips, nibbling in her impatience. I wait until people around have started to notice me, whispering behind their hands and following my gaze.

"Baby, I swear she means nothing to me! You're all I want!" I kneel before her, roses held out, words spoken far too loudly. The lunch crowd quiets, staring at us. Her face flames, her eyes darting side to side. "Blue," I whisper. When she looks at me, I give her a wink, reminding her to play along.

"Well, you should've thought of that before—before..." Blue struggles, stage fright weakening her words.

"I—I know I should have. I was weak! Nothing happened, I swear!" People have begun to nudge others all around us, pointing at my display. It's working!

"That's not what she told me!" Blue stands, shouting and pointing with such gusto I nearly forget it's all an act.

"That's because she's jealous of you! But I want nothing to do with her because I—I love you, Blue!" The words slip out. I stand on shaking legs, backing up a step at the look of pure shock in her eyes. Too far, shit, too far.

"You do?"

"Yes, more than anything. I love you, Baby Blue." I forget to yell for our audience. My words are choked, my heart pounding. She doesn't know. She thinks this is an act. Just breathe. Her eyes water on cue. Shit. Shit.

"I love you, too, Black!" She jumps into my arms, the roses crushing between us, her legs squeezing around me. My heart breaks when she kisses me. I swallow back the tears. I didn't expect this game to hurt so fucking bad.

WHAT ARE YOU DOING over break?" Allen's spittle of meatloaf juice flies dangerously close to my tray. Damn the rain keeping us inside and my tray in firing range.

"I'm going on a date with my boyfriend!" Tracie announces, her eyes alight with her conviction.

"Oh, do tell." Allen's dejection is obvious to everyone but Tracie.

"We're going to the fair, of course. I can't wait!" She does a strange little quivering jig and for the first time, I notice she is kind of cute. "What are you two doing?"

"Us?" Blue looks up from her tray, shocked. Tracie has become much more friendly with Blue since she started dating some guy from her math class. Despite Blue wanting a girlfriend, she's yet to realize Tracie is holding an olive branch out to her. "Oh...hadn't planned anything. Probably just binge anime and junk food."

"It is our forte." I nod in agreement with these plans. Colin is watching Blue strangely and a jealousy I'd never felt before rises. How odd. I've always felt strongly about Blue, sure, but I guess I've never seen anyone as a threat before.

It isn't until I'm walking out of school in search of Blue that I realize Allen was asking, not out of genuine interest, but because he wanted us all to hang out again. I am such a bad friend. Blue is branching out, maybe I should too. I'll see if Blue would be up for us all hanging over break. We'll all chill out by her pool. That'll be fun.

"Aren't you two a thing? You sure this is okay?" I hear Colin's voice as I round the corner to the back of the school where Blue and I always meet up. Colin is leaning against the brick building, hands in his pockets, eyes glued with feigned disinterest on Blue until he sees me. He juts his chin in my direction, signaling Blue that I've arrived. What the hell is going on?

"It's a long story." Is all she says before she shocks both Colin and me. Her pink-polished fingers curl into the front of his shirt and she pulls him down for a heavy kiss.

What the fuck? I'm rooted in place, my blood boiling and icing at the same time. The jealousy resurges alongside a deep ache of realization. This is over, we're over, aren't we? Whatever we were, whatever game we were playing, Blue must be done with. Blue is done with me.

Colin is released from Blue's probing mouth. He glances at me with a questioning look, no sign of apology in his gaze. She waves him off and just like that he walks away, his mysterious role now over. Blue turns to face me, unsurprised to find that I've been standing here bearing witness.

"Ready to go?" she asks as if everything is normal. She strides toward home without a care in the world.

"Hey!" I grab her arm and twist her back around. "What the—" I start to yell but then check myself. I'm so fucking pissed. I'm so damn jealous. But what right do I have in this situation? Everything up to this point has been innocent fun, a game to her. Only I have been getting caught up in the act.

"Yeah?" Blue pulls from my hold, her arms crossing over her chest.

"Wanna tell me what that was about?" I try to ask calmly, but my teeth won't unclench. My fists squeeze in an attempt to hold onto my jealous rage.

"Nothing." She shrugs, spins on her heel, and walks away from me.

I have to run to catch up. My heart is pounding, my stomach roiling. What happened? Did I do something, say something wrong? Is she over this game, thinks so little of what we've shared that she can't see how screwed up this is? Or am I overreacting and one wrong move will reveal to her how I truly feel?

"Is something wrong?" Easy. Light. Try to behave like this is normal and my heart isn't breaking.

"Nope." She's short with me. She's never short with me. The entire walk home she's silent. I don't know what to ask her, how to ask her anything. As we reach her driveway, she turns suddenly and speed walks up her front steps.

"Hey, are you—" Her front door slams, halting my question. What the hell was I going to ask, anyway? Are you mad at me? Are you dating Colin now? Are you getting caught up in the act and passive aggressively fake-dumping me?

10. Hard Truths

I give her the weekend, stewing in my confusion, jealousy, and fear. I don't text her or so much as glance out my window at her house. Out of spite, I binge through all the anime shows we were watching together. But by Monday, the first day of our week-long break from school, I can't take it anymore. This is the most we've been apart in as long as I can remember.

Blue, can we talk?

Did I do something wrong?

But my texts go unread. I send her memes, GIFs, try calling. Nothing. She hasn't blocked me on any social media, but she hasn't signed into any of them either. By Friday, I tell myself I'm over it and will just have to wait until she gets over it too. It's not like she's done being friends with me or anything. I'm sure she's missing me right about now.

Right as that thought crosses my mind, a knock sounds on the front door. Bingo. I can't help the smug smile as it forms and decide to flaunt it. She's come back to me, groveling. And I plan to punish her harshly. I'll start with reclaiming those lips of hers.

"Black, hi, is this a good time?" It isn't Blue. Damn. But it is Blue's mother. All my buried anxieties resurface. Something is definitely up. Blue's mom is normally such a workaholic she doesn't have time for anything else. It's why Blue always spends so much time at my place where it isn't so lonely. For her mother to be on my doorstep at noon on a weekday, something must have happened.

My parents are both at work, she would know that. She can't be here to see either of them. "Uh, sure. What's up?" I awkwardly walk her into the living room as if she isn't a family friend who's spent many a game night here with us.

"Well, I was hoping you could tell me. Did something happen between you two?"

We both sit at the edge of our seats, her on the sofa, me on the chair across from it, both of us unsure of ourselves.

"I...I don't really know. I saw her kissing a guy from school and now she won't talk to me." I don't tell her about the lines we've crossed, the games we've been playing. She only needs to know the recent turn of events. Everything was fine, more than fine, until I saw her with Colin. Well, she was quiet at lunch, but that's not really out of the norm. "What's been going on?"

"I see...so you haven't talked to her all week. I thought it was weird how much she was home. She's been moping around the house, not really eating or talking. Most days I find her in her room in the dark. Like all she wants to do is sleep. I even took off a few days from work to be there for her but she won't talk to me. If I didn't know any better I'd think she was either dumped or pregnant."

My eyes widen at that word. Shit. Could she be? Is it possible? We haven't exactly talked about it. I just assumed she was still taking the pill she was on to control acne and cramps. Moody, acting out, pushing me away for the first time ever...holy shit, am I gonna be a father?

Blue's mom narrows her eyes at my horrified stare. "What do you know?"

"Nothing." My underarms sting with beads of sweat. "I—I doubt that's it. I think she's just mad at me for something."

"Did you have a fight? You guys never fight."

"Not exactly. I don't know. I thought things were great, you know, like they've always been." I realize I've been scratching at my scalp in agitation and discover the skin is sore. A new nervous tick I've developed, perhaps?

"Hmm...well, can you talk to her? She won't tell me anything. You're my only hope, Black." She puts a hand on my knee, stilling its bobbing.

"Uh, sure. I can try. But she hasn't been answering my texts or calls. I even tried emailing her."

"How 'bout this, I'm gonna make her get out of the house. I'll make her go lie by the pool and get some sun. That'll be your chance to talk to her. She needs to get out of that depressing dark room anyway."

Where before I avoided looking out my bedroom window to wonder after her, I now sit glued to the pane. I stare at her bedroom window until tunnel vision blackens my gaze and narrows my focus. I search for any wiggle of her blinds to indicate she might be looking out, wondering about me. It feels like days pass before their back door opens and Blue stumbles out into the sun, hand shielding against the brightness as if she were hungover. I suppose she could be. I wouldn't know.

I have to stop myself from running to her. Halfway across my yard and I'm tiptoeing, afraid to startle her and send her scurrying back into the dark safety of her bedroom. Has she missed me? Has she thought of me? Has she felt my absence like a screaming black hole the way that I have felt hers?

Her long silken legs dangle in the water, her golden body draped at the edge of her pool. An arm covers her eyes. I stand above her for a few minutes, watching the rise and fall of her chest with each breath. My nerve is slipping. The jealous rage sidles alongside my angst. Why do I feel like I need to apologize? She's the one who broke my heart. Well, unknowingly, but still. Game or no, that was a shitty thing to do. And her ghosting me since makes it that much worse. I'd almost have preferred she tried to hang out like we used to and pretended nothing ever happened.

My body moves before my mind can make sense of how to handle this situation. I'm crawling over her, careful not to touch her, before my mind catches up. The anger at those lips being tainted by another man's push me to do what comes next.

I kiss her, angling my head to reach her lips around the arm covering her eyes. Her mouth twitches beneath mine but she does nothing more to reciprocate. She drops her arm to the side, finally acknowledging me.

"Why so blue, Blue?" It used to earn a few giggles, always guaranteed to bring a smile to her face, to melt away her worries. But her smile is tight, her eyes devoid of warmth. "Don't shut me out. You've never shut me out like this."

"Lemme see your phone." The first words she's said to me in far too long. Puzzled, I oblige and hand it over without question. "And your wallet."

Ah, now I see. I discard the contents of my pockets beside her. She tackles me into the pool where I wrap around her.

"I missed you. I thought we were gonna spend all week together." Her hair clings to my lips.

"Yeah well, I'm on so you wouldn't be getting laid anyway."

I flinch at the harshness of her voice. We might have bickered a little as children, but it's been so long since then. We always tell each other everything and have avoided many fights that way. Hearing her anger slices open an unfamiliar wound.

"So that's what this is about. You could've just talked to me. I know things have been different between us lately, but if you don't want anything like that anymore, you know I'll back off." She resists when I try to pull her to look at me.

"No, that's not... I'm sorry. I didn't mean it like that. It's some stuff I gotta figure out myself, okay?"

"No, not okay. When this all started, don't you remember what you said? You said we have to be honest with each other about everything. Please, talk to me, Baby Blue."

"I hate when you call me that." Tears choke her words. That's why she wanted to hide in the pool, to hide her tears from me.

"But I thought—"

"I know what I said!" Her hands fist in the front of my drenched shirt. "I do love it. And I hate it. I hate it so much." She kisses me, her hiccupping sobs twitching her lips rubbing against mine.

If I thought the sight of her pressing her body against Colin was painful, then seeing the anguish etched in her features is excruciating. She said things wouldn't get awkward between us. She said all we had to do was be completely honest. She said she trusts me, cares about me. I thought all of that meant we wouldn't let any of that change us, change the bond we've always shared. So, why? Why is she hiding something from me? Why is she pushing me away like this?

"Hypothetically," she pulls away to lean on her folded arms at the edge of the pool, facing away from me, "if one of us were to develop deep feelings and the other didn't, how would we be able to go back? Just go back to the way things used to be?"

Panic slices through me. And pain. She knows. I don't know how, I don't know when, but she figured it out. No. No, it makes sense. It all makes so much sense now. Colin wasn't some jab at me, but someone she's really interested in. My jealousy gave me away. Dammit. What the hell can I say to that? She's angry with me. I should've told her I'm in love with her when we made that promise. She should've known I've loved her long before we crossed the line.

It's too late. She blames herself. God, I'm such an idiot. No wonder she's pushing me away. She must think this all happened when I made love to her. She has to believe she's been leading me on unknowingly. After my jealous questioning on the way home from school, she must've figured out how I felt but misunderstood so much because of my own secrecy. What can I even say to fix this?

"Hypothetically, if that were the case," I breathe through each word carefully, pushing through the pain, holding back the tears, "I think it would be important to be open and honest with each other and to make a mutual decision of what to do about it. Whatever would happen, it wouldn't break us. No matter what, we'll always be together. Forever."

"What if it hurts too much?" Her voice is twisted in pain.

11. Poolside Confessions

I feel her words become a searing hot knife plunged deep into my chest. I want to collapse to the bottom of this pool and never resurface. Life means nothing without Blue. Black and Blue. A bruise can't be black and not blue, blue and not black.

"We'll get through it. Together. Blue, I...I can't live without you." She wails before burying her face in her folded arms. I gather her to my chest, my aching, throbbing chest.

"I'm sorry. I'm so sorry. I don't know what I was thinking when I made you promise something like that. I didn't mean for everything to get so screwed up." Her words are choked with the sobs raking through her.

"Blue, baby, please—"

"Don't. God, it hurts when you say that. Just shut up. Lemme say what I need to. Be honest, right? Well, it wasn't some drunken idea that I forced. I made sure you got drunk so that you'd agree with it. I planned it all out. And once you promised, I took advantage knowing you'd never break a promise to me." Her face rubs against my chest, bunching the wet shirt.

"It's okay, Blue. I figured as much. I don't care. I told you how much it meant to me that we shared that together."

"But that's not all of it, Black." She tries to push away from me, but I clutch her tighter. "It was only a matter of time before you lost your virginity to someone. Hell, I'm probably the only reason it hadn't happened yet. But the thought of you with someone else made me sick. *Physically sick*, Black."

I want to look at her, but she'll only allow me to hold her close. The moment I try to pull back to look at her, she tries to rip away from me. I want to soothe her, but I don't know how, I can't wrap my head around what she's saying.

"I wanted it to be with you. I *needed* it to be with you. Before it happened with someone else, before it didn't mean as much. It wasn't anything like I imagined. And I took advantage of you. You only promised to take my virginity, yet I kept coming back for more. I should've realized why the thought of you with someone else hurt me so badly. I should've known, but then I dragged you into all of this and now I'm too scared to ever let you go. I wouldn't have started all this...if only I realized it sooner. I know I should never have let myself fall in love with you. It just happened. I don't know when and I don't know what to do. Every time we touch, I want more, I want—"

"Blue." I grip her shoulders tight, forcing her to face me. "Say that again."

I must've misunderstood. I didn't hear her right. She breaks, collapsing under my hands. I hold her steady, shaking her to repeat those misheard words.

"I love you. I'm sorry, I didn't mean for this to—"

"Blue, my God, Blue, baby." My restraint breaks, tears falling at her words. I lift her, setting her on the edge of the pool.

"I'm sorry. I'm sorry," she sobs. She pulls my head to her chest and I wrap my arms around her, holding her tight against me. When I try to sit up, she clings to me.

"Look at me."

"I can't. I can't, Black."

"Look at me, baby, please." Her grip loosens. I gather her tear-streaked face in my hands, stroking away her tears with my thumbs. Her forehead is hot beneath mine. I was wrong. She's had no idea this entire time. She thought *her* feelings were unrequited. "I love you, too, Blue."

"What?" Her eyes widen, her brow furrowing.

"I'm in love with you too. I love you so much Blue, my Baby Blue."

"Black," she cries before her mouth crushes over mine. Our kisses slide in the wetness of our tears, in the pool water dripping from our hair.

I'm pushed back as she slides into the pool in front of me. She grabs the belt of my jeans and pulls me back to her. Her frantic hands rip at my belt and unfasten my jeans.

"Wait, what do we do with...how do we—when you're on?" I question against her desperate kisses. I don't know how this part works. I haven't researched enough about that yet.

"I'm not. I said that to be mean. I'm sor—"

I cut off her apology, diving my tongue in to seek that strawberry candy. She arches on her elbows from the pool ledge. Her legs wrap around my waist and I pull her bikini to the side, plunging into her and capturing the cries on her tongue. She rocks her hips with every thrust.

"I love you. I love you, Black." She moans the words and I nearly lose it.

I pump faster into her, her hips matching my pace with her own desperation. She cries my name over and over as her body convulses around me, dragging me with her. Only then do I realize that I'd been proclaiming my love for her the entire time as the words fade with the remnants of the orgasm that renders me speechless.

She's smiling when I pull her from the ledge, holding her in my arms while still buried deep within her.

After what feels like an hour later, she leaves me standing fully clothed and soaked in her pool as she runs inside to find us towels. But when she returns, her face is flushed and her brow furrowed, two large beach towels in her arms.

"Blue? What's wrong?" I don't know why it hadn't occurred to me until that moment. The blood drains from my face.

"When I went inside...my mom...she said she's glad to see we made up. I sort of told her we kind of dated."

We were so wrapped up in our own little world. The sun is still high in the sky. An entire neighborhood continues on around us. Her mother asked me to come over to talk to Blue. Of course she's been watching.

"I guess we never did tell her that was all an act."

"What was?"

"Our staged dating. She must've thought we had a breakup." I pull a towel from her grasp and discard my drenched shirt.

"About that..."

"Hm?"

"I lied about all that. I don't care about having any girlfriends. I just, I don't know, wanted to flaunt you around like you were mine in front of everyone." A blush steals over her cheeks.

"B-but the roses. I thought you—" I stutter as I stumble and kick out of my wet jeans.

"I know, I'm sorry. I was so happy when you said you loved me even though it was staged. I shouldn't have played you like that. I just wanted—"

"I meant it, you know. The whole thing might have been a game I thought you wanted to play but it was all real to me. And I guess that means I played you too. I wanted to hear you say those words even if it was fake."

Blue wraps the towel around her and I pull her to curl up with me on one of their pool lounge chairs. I should change out of these wet boxers, but I'm not ready to leave her side. Or this conversation.

"So we confessed our true feelings and neither of us figured it out." Blue's laugh sounds sad. Her wet head nuzzles my chest.

"You mean you felt that way then, too?"

"I've been in love with you for a while." Her head bobs in a nod against me.

"How long's a while?" I'll never tire of hearing those words from her lips. Would it be too soon to ask to record her saying it so that I can play it over and over?

"I don't know. Years."

"Years, my God, Blue. Years?" So all of our drunken groping, our playful games, the promise, the practice kisses, all of it was as real to her as it was to me? All this time we've been so close, I thought I knew everything there was to know about her, and yet I missed something so precious for far too long.

My jealousy resurfaces with this newfound information. "If all that is true, then what the hell was that about? Y'know...with Colin."

"Would it be cliché if I said I wanted to make you jealous?" Blue sits up to look at me, her teeth worrying her lip. "I just wanted to see if I *could* make you jealous. I guess I was testing you...I don't know how to explain it."

"So...you used Colin? You don't feel anything like that for him?"

"No. And he was kinda in on it. He asked about us while I was waiting for you the day before and I just kinda came up with it on the spot. I asked him if he would play the part for me. Since he tells us all the time about all the different girls he makes out with, I didn't think he'd mind." Blue shrugs.

I'm relieved by her confession, but the jealousy still stings. As far as I know, I was the only one to have been blessed with Blue's kiss. But now another man knows her taste. I have to tell myself that she did it for me, that if she hadn't, we probably wouldn't be having this conversation right now. Without this heartbreak, I would never have learned of her love for me.

"Say it again," I whisper into her wet hair.

"I love you, Black."

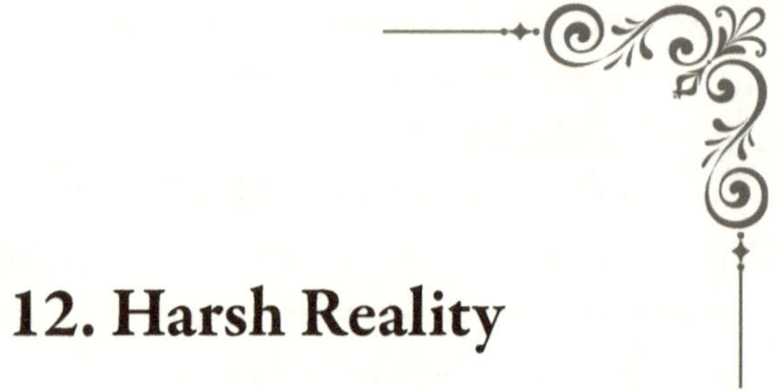

12. Harsh Reality

What happens next? Lots of make-up sex and more cuddling. Acting like a real couple. Yadda yadda ya... This fantasy fizzled out a bit. It's hard to get excited thinking about building a relationship, dating, and truly loving Blue while I sit here yearning. What was once an escape is becoming more like torture. I don't even want to think about the make-up sex. I've given myself a lifetime's worth of blue balls already.

Should I go through the day-to-day as our relationship blossoms? Or maybe I should skip to engagement, marriage, starting a family? How long would I have waited before proposing to my Baby Blue? Maybe I could do it on graduation day. Or maybe wait until college graduation. We'd go to the same college, maybe even take a lot of the same classes. We'd be as inseparable as always.

"Hey you!" Blue proclaims in that super happy put-on attitude, the mask she always wears around me.

I reach for her with my heart. I swore I felt a twitch in my fingers once, but it was so long ago now that I'm sure it was no more fantasy than my daydreams. She's checking my fluids, taking her notes, caressing my hand, my leg, my shoulder in her examinations.

I love you, Blue, I tell her, telepathically caressing her. But of course, if these lips move, if they ever have, I couldn't proclaim such love for my nurse. I think she knows I've given up. Or rather, never had the desire to try. I'm fairly content in my daydreams. If I were granted the chance at a second life, I wouldn't have the pleasure of Blue's daily presence. I wouldn't have the freedom to fantasize about our lives together. I'd be forced to build a new one, one likely without her in it at all.

So why should I try to put all of my energy into getting these stiff limbs to move? Why attempt to connect brain to mouth, to body? I have everything I'd ever need, sitting right on this bed and reading to me in her sweet honeyed voice.

"Morning, Tracie." Blue stops reading when my other regular nurse enters my gray little room.

"Hey, kiddo. How're you doing?" Tracie lays a soothing hand on Blue's shoulder. "Are you ready for this?"

But Blue doesn't answer, just dips her head, a tremble on her lips. If I could, I'd cock my head to one side. I'd reach for Blue and caress her worries away. It has something to do with me. Something's happening. Maybe there's a plug somewhere, a drug pumping into me that's been keeping me alive. Maybe today's the day it stops.

"Have you told him?" Tracie gets to work on removing cords and lines, machines coming in and going out. My eyes ever glued to Blue, she turns to me, the mask sliding into place.

"Alie," She inhales deeply. "Today's moving day. We're gonna take you..."

The words falter from her lips, her face twisting as tears threaten to spill. Ah, so that's it. I'll be stuck in some smaller, darker hole. An assisted living hellhole, the kinds where a sweet

Angel of Death might grant me mercy. If I need one. Without my Blue, perhaps the tiniest will to live will finally leave me. And it can be over.

No one speaks to me during the move. It's a strange sensation to be strapped to a bed, bumping and swaying down the road. The movement after so much stagnation has my heart pounding. If I were hooked up to the same fully loaded machines as in the dank hospital room, I imagine a few heart rate alarms would be frantically screeching right about now.

I'm moved from my hospital bed onto a normal bed, this one a little larger, a full, perhaps. We've arrived at some house, something my blurry eyes cannot make sense of. But the room I'm settled into is about the same small size as the hospital I've been evicted from. The walls are pale pink, the curtains a feminine lacy number of faded white. A bookshelf sits in one corner, the titles too blurry to decipher. The room is set up with fewer gadgets than I was hooked up to before.

Once I'm hooked up, plugged in, and settled, the moving crew of blurry faceless men disappears. Tracie and Blue busy themselves around me, tucking blankets, checking numbers, taking notes.

By now, I'd have settled into fantasies of us, in a different time, a different place. But the strain of this move prevents me from settling into the ease of my daydreams. They talk between themselves, planning out my new life for me. I couldn't be bothered to listen, to care.

"Alie!" Blue suddenly proclaims, startling my heart into a frenzy. "I'm so sorry!" Trembling fingers swipe at my cheeks. Am I crying?

"Shit, he's probably scared. I'm gonna head out and give you guys some space. You should explain what's going on, kiddo. I know you're scared it'll be like last time, but he deserves to know."

Tracie leaves, Blue's fat tears wobble in her too-big, too-sad eyes. I love her presence. But I fucking hate when she looks at me like that.

"Alie, sweetheart, listen." Blue strokes my arm, careful to avoid the lines of machines that force me to live. "This is...we're...you're home—my house. I brought you to my house. This way, we'll always be together. It'll be easier for me to take care of you now."

I think that was supposed to make me feel better. This is the burden that I am. What the hell does Blue want with me? What the fuck am I supposed to do with this news? Why is it her responsibility to care for me?

I love you, Blue.

I love you.

Kill me.

Not much has changed. Mornings start with a sponge bath, much harder with just Blue to lift and twist me. I'm fed baby food mush at the same exact times. Bitter crushed pills spoil the sweet potato mash that accompanies every dinner. She reads to me. I promptly fall into a dreamless sleep. And another week, a month, a season goes by.

13. All Things Blue

"I ...love..." Raspy words rattle from my lips. "Love... Blue..."

"Blue? You love blue?"

This puzzles her. And excites her. But my error becomes clear. She has no idea of my name for her. The next day, her shirt is a dark blue, her nails turquoise. A few weeks later, my bed sheets are swapped from black to blue. The lacy curtains disappear, navy blue drapes appearing in their place.

"Hey, kiddo. Sorry I'm late. Mr. Gerkins coded today. It was such a mess. Ninety years old and the family had it on file he had to be resuscitated, can you believe it? His chest was a damn mess by the time they finally decided to let him go." Tracie comes by sometimes to help get me into a wheelchair, take me out like a dog needing a walk.

I want to feel the sun. I can't remember what it feels like. But the heavy clouds and stiff breeze shatter those dreams.

"What the hell are you wearing, by the way?" Tracie comments on Blue's ridiculous appearance. Her blue nails, all blue outfit, she even added blue extensions into her black curls, the straight blue streaks dangling several inches longer than the rest of her hair.

"He said he loves blue. So I wear blue every day, bought all kinds of new things for his room. I'm planning to repaint it blue soon. Once I have some spare time. And can get some help moving things around to do it."

"Count me out. My back's acting up again. We had this lady come in for kidney problems a few days ago and when I went to help move her for a scan, *pop*! The last thing I need is to do more lifting and moving. You sure you aren't going a little overboard? I still haven't heard him say a thing, not even a grunt."

"He was talking in his sleep last night. I swear I heard it. But by the time I got to his room, nothing."

"Honey," Tracie starts to say. Blue always gets like this. She hears words I'm not capable of uttering, sees twitches I'm not capable of making, sees emotions I've long since forgotten how to feel. I managed to whisper my love for her once, and she grossly misunderstood.

"I dreamt he was talking again, just like before. It felt so real." My wheelchair is stopped. Faint sobbing sounds from behind me. In the branches above, I see a bird I should know the name of, but like everything else, the memory escapes me. The black bird with its long fan of a tail peers down at me. I wag my tongue at it, taunting the creature.

"Why don't you come out with me tonight? That new intern I told you about, Chelsea, she'd love to come over and sit with Al. She's such an overachiever that you'll probably come home while she's in the middle of giving him a mani-pedi."

"Shh! I know you mean well but—"

"No buts. Just do it. Nobody is telling you to move on, I'm just saying to let loose a little. Have a dance, let a stranger buy you a drink. You're looking ten years older, hon. Come out, have fun with me."

That's a daydream I don't like toying with. I've been living in Blue's house for quite some time now. And I'm sure of it. She lives alone, no husband to match the glittering diamonds she wears. Tracie pushes for girls' night out almost every weekend, urging Blue to move on. I wonder if her husband left her because of me. Or if he's been out of the picture for some time and I became something of a project to fill the hole he left behind.

There's another idea I toy with, one that makes me feel a little better about being Blue's burden. What if her husband is the reason I'm in the state I'm in? I like to think he was a drunk who ran me over or caused an accident that did this to me. I like to think the accident killed him and now, out of some twisted guilt, Blue tries nursing me to health to atone for her drunken husband's sin.

Blue looks so dejected by Tracie's denial that by the time we return from our stroll, I've worked up the gumption to try again.

"I..." I cough, a growling of an attempt but it does the trick. Tracie is tucking the wheelchair into the corner, oblivious.

"Alie, what is it? Speak to me!" Blue rushes to my side, abandoning my legs where she'd been cocooning them into the new blue blankets. "Tracie, get over here!"

Tracie looks over her shoulder, a look crossing her face that is half worry and half exasperation.

"I love...Blue. You." Dammit. Close enough. But the way Blue's face lights up—finally, she's been validated. She's grabbing Tracie, shaking her, crying into her shoulder.

"You see! He's talking again. He wants more blue. Please help me paint, it'll make him so happy!" Blue's cries warm my heart, but her misunderstanding crushes me. Tracie stares at me with such a probing look that I want to turn away.

"Al, you're talking about her, aren't you?"

Tracie understands me! Yes! Blue, my Blue, I love my Blue. I open my mouth, chewing on words that won't come to me. Blue pins me with her tear-streaked face.

"B...lue."

"He's calling you Blue."

"Me? I'm Blue? Is she right, Alie?" Blue leans in close, her lips above mine. I wonder if her kiss would taste like the strawberry candy I've always fantasized about.

"I love you." I did it! I said it! It isn't until the words I'd worked so hard to speak have left my neglected lips that I bother to think about the consequences. Why would I say such a thing? Blue sobs against my chest and I realize what I've done. But the sweet smile on Tracie's mouth makes me question my insecurity.

Tracie wraps my arms around Blue, helping me to hold her. She waits there for a few minutes, allowing me to hold my love for the first time. And then she eases my arms back to my sides, kisses my forehead, then the top of Blue's head, and leaves.

"I love you, too," Blue sobs against my chest. But of course, there's no way she could mean it the way that I do. Is it the love of friendship, is that what I am to her? She's ecstatic that I've managed to speak, to prove that I could speak. The words I said didn't matter. I could've said my ass itched and she'd have been just as happy.

Or so I thought.

Blue sits up, wiping at her face despite more tears that quickly follow. I notice a tremble racking through her. And then she abruptly twists, laying her upper body over me, her lips crushing over mine.

I've never had such a vivid and powerful imagination like this. I never dream. Has my mind become stronger, like a man who's lost sight gaining super hearing? Soft shaking hands frame my face, holding my mouth to hers. I've died and managed to stumble into heaven. Yeah, that makes sense.

I return her kiss the best I can, reveling in this strange hallucination. I feel a strange sensation all through my body, tingling vibrations sparking in my fingertips, in my toes. Is her kiss magic?

Blue doesn't read to me. I'm fed the bitter pill powder that makes me sleep. But instead of easing into another night of dreamless sleep with the soothing voice of her reading those blasted romance novels to me, she does something else. She joins me in the bed.

I drift off with the feel of her nestled beside me, the weight of her slender arm gripped tightly around my waist, her soft breath on my bare shoulder. It becomes a new routine. Blue sleeps beside me every night, wrapped around me in a tender embrace. She's begun working with me every day, urging more words from my throat. I read those damned romance novels to her, sounding like some five-year-old stuttering over every word.

One day as I'm reading to her, she sits staring at me, enthralled by my steady voice. She forgets to turn the page. I keep reading the last sentence over and over, waiting for her to catch on, laughing to myself at her obliviousness. And then it happens.

I reach up with my right hand, briefly grazing the back of her hand, before it plops back to my lap, lifeless once more.

"Alie!" she squeals, pinning my head to her chest. I feel like a child being congratulated at every step I take.

"Thank you, Blue." My words have returned to me. The stuttering five-year-old disappearing.

"Oh, Alie. I'm so happy!"

"Black," I tell her. I want to hear her say my name. I've always hated Al, Alfred, or any version of my real name. That much I know.

"Huh? Black what?"

"Call me Black. Black and Blue. That's us." My explanation is shit.

"Black and Blue." A look of worry etches her sweet features. "Black, okay. I like it."

"Say it again." I would cup the side of her face if I could. The fingers of my right hand twitch.

"I love you, Black." Her profession of love startles me. I sit there blinking lamely at her. And then I'm crying. Those lips do taste like strawberries, I'm excited to discover. She's showering me with kisses, swiping at my tears with her thumbs.

She stops giving me the pills that make me drowsy not long after that. We stay up late in the night talking about the novels she reads. There's the shadow hanging over us of the truth, the story behind my situation that I want to ask her. But something holds me back. There's a fear I can't place associated with learning the reason behind everything.

Later that night, something happens. I blame those books. And the warmth of her body beside me. When I drift off into the fantasy of our first time, the illusion of best friends making a promise, the usual erection that perks up at the daydream goes one step further. Blue shifts in her sleep, her leg draping over me, grazing against the cock that aches for her. I choke off the moan by sinking teeth into my bottom lip. The waves crash over me, tears pricking my eyes with the intensity. An uncomfortable mess coats my thighs and the thin boxers Blue had slid into place only hours before.

I'm fucking terrified when it's time for my morning sponge bath. The steaming water sits at the ready on the table beside me. She's dipping and squeezing the washcloth, smoothing the hot limp thing up each of my arms.

"Wait." My voices trembles. She stops, watching, waiting, her hands gripping the sheets, ready to lift away and discover my secret.

"What's wrong? Your face is all red."

"I-it just happened. I didn't mean to..." Happy that I can at least turn my head, I face away, waiting for the source of my humiliation to be discovered. The sticky mess had hardened and crusted against my thighs, the residue pulling at hairs as she attempts to strip me. "I'm sorry."

She inhales sharply. I feel my face heat even more. The soiled boxers are eased from my legs and the tepid washcloth scrubs at the residual mess.

"Somebody had a sexy dream last night." I'm grateful there's no teasing in her voice. But it sounds strange, tinged with something I can't place.

"I'm sorry," I whisper again.

"Don't be, Black." I can't stifle the tremor as she begins cleaning the mess from far too sensitive areas. "Tell me about it."

"I don't remember," I lie. "I must've dreamed about the last book you made me read."

"Yeah? Stacy get you all hot and bothered?" Blue teases. But I don't remember the female lead's name. I don't remember anything about any of those books I read to her. And they're usually pretty tame, no detailed sexy scenes beyond a passionate kiss. But the last few have been a little racier. It has to be because of those books.

"Sure," I mumble half-heartedly. Dammit, how much of a mess did I make? Her hands are lingering too close for too long. I can already feel the traitorous lump of useless flesh engorging.

"Tell me about it. Please." Startled by the strange sound of her voice, I look at her. Her cheeks are flushed, her gaze focused on her hands. Delicate fingertips whisper across the head.

"Fuck." The word slips from my clenched teeth. "Blue."

I meant it as a warning, that her hands were in dangerous territory. But it backfires. She abandons the rag, her hand wrapping around me.

"Were you thinking of me?" She strokes her hand up and down, slow, gentle.

"Ah! Yes!"

"What were you thinking about?" She pumps her hand faster. What is happening? What the fuck is happening?

"Blue!"

"Tell me." She squeezes.

"Sex!" I cry at the onslaught.

"Tell me!" Her hand stills, pumps once, stops again.

I ramble, confessing to the fantasy of taking her virginity, of fulfilling a promise made back in an imaginary youth. Her

hand pumps faster, satisfied with my confession. I come in vio-
lent bursts, making a new mess on my thighs.

"Sorry, I'm sorry," I pant, humiliated, sated, and spent.

Blue kisses me, a sweet, tender caress.

14. Thank God for Little Black Dresses

Not a word is spoken about the incident later when Tracie stops by to help with another walk. I think my ability to talk unnerves her. She mostly yammers about work with Blue, only ever directing a few pleasantries my way. And always in such an annoyingly condescending tone that makes me grow to loathe her.

"How's Black today?" she coos, taking to my requested nickname with ease, thankfully.

I gave up trying to impress her with the strength of my voice, quickly discovering her disinterest. But I am content in the friendship she provides Blue. Just like my fantasy world, I have to remind myself I'll never be enough to satisfy her. She needs people like Tracie in her life. She needs others.

That night, Blue comes to my room dressed in a way I've never seen before. She wears a tight black cocktail dress, tall stiletto heels. Her curly hair seems extra voluminous. Dark seductive makeup highlights her features. She turned Tracie's invitation down, I could've sworn. But that outfit says otherwise. That outfit says Blue is looking for the touch of another.

"Blue..." Worry and lust spike my pulse.

"What do you think?" She spins once, slow, giving me a mouthwatering view. I want to cry.

"You're breathtaking." A blush blooms over her cheeks, down her neck. The cocktail dress plunges between her breasts, flaunting a cleavage I can't remember ever setting my eyes on. The dress hugs her beautiful curvaceous body in such a way that I find myself angry at the world. At the designer who would create a dress so perfectly suited to her body. That any man will fall at her heels the moment she saunters in to wherever Tracie is meeting her tonight.

"Tracie is always saying I should do this, let loose at little. I thought maybe I could give it a try." Is this Blue asking for my blessing? Is this a tease, a reward of eye candy before she leaves me to my jealousy for the rest of the night?

I find anger twitching my hand, fingers desperately wanting to clench into a fist. I'm supposed to say something. Something like *sure, have fun. Don't stay out too late.* Be supportive, right? She's been so much for me. She deserves it. But I can't bring myself to say anything.

"Oh, be right back. I forgot something!" I can't ignore the excitement in those words. She's wanting. She's excited from wanting. The thrill of tonight's itinerary must be bubbling within her.

But I'm confused when she returns, a chilled six-pack of beer in her freshly manicured hands. Am I supposed to sip beers while she's out? Is she so excited that she's forgotten I can wiggle a few fingers every once in a while, nothing more? Or perhaps Tracie's intern will be here shortly to help me get drunk on these beers while Blue paints the town.

"I know it's risky, but a few beers shouldn't hurt, right?" Blue pops the top, sitting at the edge of my bed and tilting her mop of curls back as she sips the golden liquid.

This beautiful sexy goddess who is my guardian angel is nervous. I can see it in the shaking hands clutching the brown bottle, in the wiggling of her glossy pink lips. When she attempts to help me drink the beer, it spills down my neck in a fizzing trickle.

"Shit, sorry." She avoids looking into my eyes as she wipes up the mess. The little bit of beer I managed to swallow tastes nostalgic, familiar. I know I've tasted this brand before. I may have even loved it most. Why can I recall the taste of beer but nothing else? How long has it been since this accident? Was it an accident? Or maybe I was born this way. Maybe I'm some lab rat, first of my kind to undergo some surgery that made me capable of speech. Maybe I can't remember anything because I have no memories.

Who is this beautiful, sexy nurse who brought me to her home? This incredible woman who cleans up after me, pushes me to progress, whispers coos of love?

Music surrounds us, echoing off the walls, tingling my subconscious with its familiarity. Songs I recognize but can't place when, where, how. Blue sets a small speaker on the table beside my bed, the song seductive, slow.

"Black, I want you to look at me. Don't look away." Blue stands on those tall heels, her hips swaying with the music. Her hands trail up her thighs, over her flat stomach, caressing rounded hips. My throat is dry.

I'm hard, painfully hard. And humiliated, confused. She cups her breasts, her head falling back, her hips ever swaying.

She spins on her heels, turning her back to me. Then she's bending over, peeking over her shoulder at me, winking. She flips her hair up.

"Blue…" I'm afraid where this is going. What is she planning? Those red painted nails glisten as she reaches behind her, easing the zipper of her dress down. The cocktail dress pools at her feet. A new song plays, this one as sexy as the last. She turns to face me, to confront me with the secrets she'd kept hidden beneath her clothes all this time.

Red lace cups perfect breasts, a matching red thong painted over those sinful hips. Her fingertips trace the lines of lace, dipping between her cleavage, stroking low on her belly. And I'm panting. Her heels plop off as she crawls from the foot of the bed. She straddles me, the red lace sharpening before my blurry eyes.

Her breasts press to my face as she leans over me. I bend my head forward as far as I can manage and am just able to reach the swell of her breast with the tip of my tongue. She gasps, sitting on my lap, the beer materializing in her hand. She gulps at it, her throat taunting me. My inability to touch her, to pull off that taunting lace brings tears to my eyes.

"Take it off." My strained words bark at her.

"I will." Her smile is dangerous, a wide grin of teeth sharper than I can ever remember seeing. "But first…"

Blue tips her head back, draining the beer bottle. Her lips are on mine, cold and firm. And then her hands tip my head back as her tongue eases my lips apart. Beer spills into my mouth. I gulp greedily at the liquid she offers me.

"More," I beg. She opens another beer, filling her mouth and passing it to me. God, it feels so good to have the sparkling beer on my tongue again. The alcohol already dances in my blood. How long has it been since I've been drunk? Have I ever been drunk?

Her hips grind against me. I'm too drunk to stifle the moan, too drunk to bother trying to wrap my head around what the hell is happening. The bra disappears, perfect breasts, as perfect as they were in my fantasy, press against my lips. She cries out at the cool touch of my tongue on her burning flesh.

"Black, oh, it feels so good."

I lap at her, nibbling the engorged nipple between my chattering teeth. Her hands fist in my hair, her feverish body pressing against me. The boxers I wear, the only clothes she puts on me each night, are not enough protection from her pumping hips.

"Careful, close," I choke out from where she has my face buried between her breasts.

"It's too much. I can't wait." She yanks the pillows propping up my head, tossing them to the floor. Her mouth devours mine. My limp hands twitch with the desire to touch her. I feel her fingers toying with my boxers, unbuttoning the hole, easing my cock out of it.

And then this goddess, my nurse, my love, this mystery woman that is the only reason I cling to life, towers over me. I can't tilt my head down to see what she's doing, but I know. Her eyes bore into mine as she slides down onto my cock, easing me into her so fucking slowly it's driving me insane. I can feel the rub of the red lace and it's almost too much.

"Blue, God, Blue." I want to grip her hips, hold her steady before it's too late.

"Sorry, I'm sorry. It's too good." Her kiss is madness, her hips pumping along with the insanity.

"I'm going to—" But she eats my words. And I'm coming, the tight slick heat of her too much for my sensitive body.

"Black, fuck, yes!" Her body convulses on top of me. Her mouth hot on my ear.

"Oh, Blue…" I whimper as the residual waves shoot through me. She lies on top of me, the full length of that gorgeous body blanketing me.

"Let me know if I'm hurting you. I can get off," she pants, her breath hot on my neck.

"A second time? So soon?" I tease. Her body shakes with her chuckle. I suck in a breath at the sensations. Blue sits up on her elbows, dark shadowed eyes staring down at me. A jingle sounds between us as I feel a tiny *thunk* of something hitting my chest. How could I forget? Blue has always worn a man's wedding band around her neck. In my lust I didn't see the painful reminder of her marriage. She sees the change in my gaze, which I avert to the wall.

"You want to know about this, don't you?" She leans to one side, dangling the ring above my face. "But that's a tale for another day. For now, just know it's been seven years since I've had this."

Her hips pump, once. My moan brings a smile to her swollen lips. She pulls the necklace off her neck, removes the rings from her finger and abandons them on the table.

"I wonder how long it's been for me." Or maybe I just lost my virginity.

"Just as long, I can assure you." I want to ask her how she could *assure me*, how could she know anything like that about me? But her body distracts me. She sits up, leaning back with her hands propped behind her, wrapped around my knees. And her hips are pumping slow, steady.

"I want to touch you." My words reveal far too much despair than I'd intended. But Blue finds a way. She leans over me, propping my limp arm up by placing my elbow on her thigh. Her hands guide mine over her breast, kneading my fingers into the soft skin. I successfully pinch her nipple with her assistance and nearly lose myself a second time.

"I'm gonna—" Blue cries out.

"Don't!" But it's too late. She's writhing, and I follow her, crying out at the intense pleasure.

"Black. Oh, how I've missed you," she whimpers, so softly I nearly miss it. Her words confuse me but somehow, I know I wasn't meant to hear those words.

It isn't until much later that night, as I settle into a half-sleep beside her that it occurs to me. She dressed up like that just for me. She was never intending to go out with Tracie, she merely took her advice but turned a night *out* into a night *in*. With me. Oh, Blue, my sweet, lovely Blue.

What did I ever do to deserve you?

15. Hard Work and Heavy Goodbyes

An intense regimen of physical therapy begins. But it takes years before I finally stand on my own two feet. And even longer before I take my first steps unassisted. Blue's daughter came to visit me a few times in the beginning, a beautiful clone of her mother. The little girl doesn't say much but watches me with such a probing intensity that it feels like she could see into my mind and discover truths lost to me.

The moment she walked into the room that first time, as I struggled to feel the floor beneath my feet with the unfamiliarity of my bulk weighted upon them, I felt the strength leave already weak knees. If I had met Blue one day, not found myself awake and cared for by her, not daydreaming an alternate reality where Blue was always a part of it, but truly had the blessed opportunity to meet Blue, this must be how it would have felt.

I loved her the moment my dead eyes met her vibrant reflection of her mother's. I wanted to teach her to dance while play pretending she was a princess. I wanted to watch her grow and thrive. Threaten her prom date about strict curfew then smile knowingly when she came home an hour late. Or try to and not ground her, try to be that parent who remembers what it's like to be a child, a teen, a person discovering themselves.

I yearned to give her the talk. Not the awkward sex talk no one deserves to suffer through at the hands of their parents, the real talk. The one about life and longing and what it all means. Does it all mean something, what can she do with her life, what is the purpose, the point?

But I don't know anything about life. The urge to part with any of my knowledge, despite my utter lack of ability or credibility, alludes me. Should I not instead feel jealousy that she is the product of Blue and another man? Why does seeing this little girl invoke such odd thoughts? Why is it that her cold and curious stare strikes new strength into these creaking knees?

I wonder where the girl lives, why I haven't seen her often and why Blue doesn't talk about her. But the girl gives me this strange encouragement. It was after the first time I remember meeting her that I truly began to make progress. It was after meeting her that Blue scheduled more rigorous therapy sessions. And it's that girl and her probing stare I think of when I struggle to take the next step.

Five years have passed since I came to live with Blue. She tells me it's been ten years since the accident. As my abilities improved I find Blue more open to telling me what happened that day.

"You were in a car accident with your parents." They were visiting from their retirement home in Florida. I was driving them home from the airport when the drunk driver swerved over the yellow line. Mother died in the accident. But father survived, dying of a heart attack a year later. I don't remember any of it. Surely my father had visited me before he died. Surely, he was the one who was paying for my hospital bills before I became Blue's burden.

"When did we meet? Were you working the night I was brought into the hospital?"

"Was I—" Blue turns to me on our stroll around the neighborhood, confusion painting her beautiful features. She's more open with me about my accident. But not about her. Any questions regarding us, her daughter, any kind of past especially relating to those wedding rings she still wears, and I get nothing.

My place in this world is my constant thought. When I began to talk and walk again, the doctors called it miraculous. When my strength returned to my body and I felt more and more human, I felt less and less one with purpose. In my vegetative state, I existed only to burden Blue and please myself with fantasies of her. But now?

Ten years of recovery, no memories have returned to me. I don't know my skill set. My education or experience. The first time I looked in a mirror, I couldn't comprehend what I saw. An old man stared back at me, not the twenty-something I thought I'd see. Blue had just given me a haircut and trim. She wanted to show me the handsome look she claimed she'd given me.

A forty-year-old graying, wrinkled face appeared before my eyes. Forty years old. No skill set. No known education or experience. Parents dead because of my driving failure. My body marred with the scars of what I'd survived.

I looked at Blue, seeing the beautiful young woman standing in the mirror beside the old man that is me. And nothing makes any sense. This young nurse has cared for me, cared *about* me for all these years. But why? Is this some twisted syndrome I've never heard about? A syndrome for nurses, whose caring goes too far with her weakest patient, a devotion turned obsession disguised as love?

I want to ask her how old she is, but I fear the answer. Early twenties, surely. No, a little older. Her daughter is maybe ten. But she could've had her young, fifteen perhaps. No, because then she wouldn't have been old enough to be working in the hospital when I was first admitted. Thirty could work. She's a youthful thirty. Devoted to an old man for no discernable reason.

"Don't you like it?" Blue asked, drawing my thoughts back to the haircut she'd given me. There's so much gray in my medium-brown hair. The style she'd given me, a faux hawk of sorts, was likely her attempt to make me look younger. She'd trimmed my facial hair to look like a few days past needing a shave. The white streaks in the black scruff ruin the youthful appearance she'd tried to force onto this old man's face.

In my head, I was just graduating high school, the love of my life, Blue, beside me. I conjured those fantasies based off of nothing but my love for the young woman who cared for me. How foolish this empty head of mine was to believe I was her age. How foolish to believe I had found my true love in that hospital room.

I know what I have to do.

BABY BLUE,

I want to thank you for everything you've done for me. I want you to know that I love you far more than I should. I love you so much.

I'm so sorry for the burden I have been. I should've tried harder for you. I should've worked to get back to health and out of your life sooner. But I had no will to live, no desire to fight what happened to me. You were so devoted, so nurturing. When I became your personal burden, when you moved me into your house and began taking full responsibility for me, I had to do it for you.

But I wasn't trying hard enough. I took ten years away from you. Ten years from your husband. From you daughter. From your life. I don't know what you wanted from me, what guilt bound you to me, but I want you to know that you're free now. I can't imagine what financial burden I must be leaving you with.

I saw the life insurance policy on me. I just happened to see it on the table. And I saw a few of the medical bills. I'm going to make it look like an accident. You have to burn this letter so no one can find out the truth. I'm an old man. With no memories, no skills. I don't even know if I graduated high school. So much has changed in the ten years I've been a baby learning how to eat and shower by myself all over again. I'll never be able to work off my debts to you.

You're still so young. After my debts are paid with the insurance, you can start over. You can go anywhere. You can be with your daughter again. Maybe return to your husband, if that's something you want. Those necklaces you always wear...there must be a reason you can't take them off.

Thank you for everything you've done for me. I'm so sorry that I'm an ungrateful bastard. It's far too late for an old man like me to enjoy this second chance at life that you've given me. It's unfair what I've done to you, what I've taken from you with nothing to offer in return. At least in this way, hopefully the slate can be wiped clean. The bills paid, your burden gone. This is your second chance, don't waste it like I have.

I don't expect you to forgive me. In fact, I hope you don't. I hope you hate me. And I hope that hate pushes you forward, pushes you not to think about me.

I love you. I love you, my Baby Blue.

Black

16. Playground Confessions

She's probably woken up and found the letter by now. Or maybe she's sleeping in, her body still tingling from my touch. I made sweet love to her, knowing full well it was good-bye. I haven't quite figured out exactly how to make it look like an accident. I have to time it right. Not too long that she'd do something stupid like send police to look for me. And not too soon that she learns of my death after the fact, with no time to read and destroy the letter.

A day should be more than enough. I could find some woods, wander in and wait for a wild animal. I could drown in a lake, stage it to look like I'd gone for a leisurely swim. I could fall into traffic. That seems almost fitting, a car putting all this in motion. A car ending it.

I swing at the school in the twilight of early morning. The school, not far from Blue's home and a frequent stop on our regular walks, was the basis for my fantasy. I can see the fake teenage versions of us that I'd created, attempting to play a made-up game of train. A game I'd likely never played and probably made up after watching TV over the years bound to that bed.

What should I do with one more day to live? Maybe I should find my parents' graves and say goodbye. Well, I guess it would be more like see you soon than goodbye. Maybe I can swing into the hospital that became the location of my first memories, the place I met Blue. But no, I might run into Tracie there and derail this whole plan.

A day of sulking in my loneliness, a day of questioning my decision. No, I can't wait much longer. I need to do this soon. If I can't time it right so that Blue has enough time to burn the letter, then I can at least make it so my body isn't found right away. A fake drowning accident might be the best bet.

A set of headlights drives slowly by. The day is beginning, people starting to wake up and run errands. I need to get moving, reduce chances for witnesses. But I want to see the sunrise, feel the warm caress one last time. So much time was spent in the darkness of a hospital room. I'm not ready for eternal darkness, not without one last kiss from the sun.

"Black!" A scream echoes in the trees behind me. I bolt to my feet in terror. She found me. Shit. Shit.

I can just make out the shadow running toward me from the parking lot, a running car behind her, the door open, the headlights shining.

"Black! Wait, please!" She's screaming, sobbing, hysterical. Fuck. Fuck. Should I run? I should run. If only I could actually run. But her screams. The houses close behind me have lights coming on. Witnesses. Shit.

I back up, ready to attempt to bolt but unsure where to go, what to do. Blue launches into my arms, knocking me to the ground and purging the air from my lungs. Fists pound my chest, tears soak my shirt.

"You asshole! You asshole!" she screams.

"I'm sorry. I'm so sorry," I whisper into her hair, choking on the words. I never thought I'd get to hold her again. In my weakened state, I cling to her, stilling her assailing fists.

"You can't leave us! You can't!"

Us?

"It's the only way, Blue."

"I don't fucking care about the bills!" She sits up, pinning me to the ground beneath her. "How could you even think to do this to me? To her!" Her fists slam into my chest, forcing me to gasp for air.

"Blue—"

"Shit. I'm sorry. I'm sorry. Are you okay?" She's nuzzling my face, kissing my cheeks. Perhaps she'll kill me here. A robbery gone wrong. Insurance will cover that, as long as she gets away with staging it.

We lie there, the sun beginning to lighten the sky. She cries softly as I stroke her hair. This is why I left a letter. I knew she would never agree to something like this. I know it's selfish to do this to her. It's selfish not to work hard to make it all up to her. I'm not the man she must've imagined when she spent so much of her life working hard for my recovery.

"Tell me, Black," she whimpers. "Did I force you to live? Did you want to let go but held on for me?"

"I don't know." But I do know. This is what I need to do. Be honest. Like our fake promise of years past, from a past that never existed. "I don't know who I was. Who I am. Who I'm supposed to be. Maybe I did want to let go. I don't know what kept me alive. I don't know what gave me the will to live. All I know is that over the years of you caring for me, I fell in love."

"I'm sorry. It's all my fault. I'm such a coward."

"How? What are you talking about, Blue?" I urge her to sit up, to look at me in the growing light.

"A year after the accident, you started to talk. You could move your hand. Do you remember any of that?"

I try to think back but I can't remember being admitted to the hospital. I don't remember anything from my past. I can't even remember meeting Blue. One day I was just there in the hospital and Blue was beside me, smoothing a cloth down my arm. "No, I don't remember anything like that."

Her brows furrow at my words, her lip trembling. "I was cocky. I was stupid. You were asking who you were, who I was, what happened. I told you everything. I thought you would suddenly remember. I thought it would click and we'd go home, and you could walk again, and everything would go back to normal."

"But it didn't." Clearly something happened.

"I don't know what happened. You just started seizing or something. But the doctors said it wasn't a seizure. You were convulsing. It must have been too much of a shock, learning the truth like that. And when you woke up a few days later, it was like nothing ever happened. You couldn't talk anymore or move your hand. And it was like you didn't recognize me again."

"I'm so sorry, Blue." I hold her as she cries, her face buried against my chest. Thank God it's Sunday and no kids will be circling us to poke and prod with sticks. The sun peeks over the horizon, stretching the school playground in long shadows, pushing out the night's chill from the air.

"I've been too scared it would happen again. I've kept the truth from you all this time, terrified to lose you like that. But it seems I'm going to lose you one way or another."

"Blue, I—"

She pulls from my embrace, sitting beside me, her eyes to the bluing sky. Her mouth forms silent words I can't decipher. Blue pulls her necklace off, frees the ring, then hands it to me.

"Put it on," she says simply. Confused, I slip the ring on my finger. It looks normal. It's a little loose, but it feels *right*.

A rustling sound comes from her pocket before a piece of paper is pressed into my hand. I stare down at the document, confused at the words printed there.

"Read it. Out loud to me," she commands softly, eyes never leaving the sky.

"Alfred James Wilson—I...I thought my middle name was Lee?"

"Keep going, what's the other name?"

"Natalie Anne Colins. This is a marriage license. It's from over twenty years ago. I don't understand. Who—"

"What's my name, Black?"

"I... Blue—no, your real name. Angelica. Angel. Isn—" But Blue is shaking her head. Her face twisting in anguish when I say what I'd thought was her name.

"You used to call me Lee. My name is Natalie."

"You...you're my wife." I say the obvious. Silent tears streak down her face.

"But then, who's Angelica?"

"She's..." Blue inhales, steeling herself for whatever she's about to say. My heart pounds. My mind desperately trying to piece it all together. I got my own name wrong, not just hers. "Angelica is our daughter."

Our daughter.

I have a daughter. That little girl. She's my daughter. I have a child. With Blue, my wife of over twenty years. I didn't remember my own wife. My own child.

"Oh God, Blue." I clutch her against me, sobbing as my heart breaks at the realization of her own pain, at my daughter's pain. "She's only ten. There's still time. I still have time. Who's she been living with? Where's she been all this time?"

Blue stiffens in my embrace. Hands framing my face, she coos softly, "Black, listen to me." Her eyes close. "Angel is twenty-two, not ten. And she's—she's not here. She's in Africa right now."

"What? But I just saw her not that long ago. She was just a child. She can't be that old. Wait, that marriage license. Is the date right? You would've been a child when we married. This can't be right. None of this—"

She kisses me, soothing my panic with her sweet, soft lips. My mind is screaming, my blood roaring in my ears. And she keeps kissing me. My wife is kissing me. My wife of over twenty years. The mother of my daughter.

"Breathe, my love. You have to breathe. I can't lose you again. I can't go through that again." Blue's anguish settles my frantic mind. Be strong, for her. For them.

"Blue...I know it's scary, but I need to know. Everything." I grip her shoulders. The sun sparkles in her eyes. Traffic sounds reach my ears, notifying me of the world that has woken up.

"I know. I know. If it becomes too much, we have to stop. I'll tell you everything, but we have to take it slow." She continues at my nod. "How old do you think I am, Black?"

"Barely thirty." But as I say the words, it suddenly doesn't mesh. There's salt in the pepper of her hair that I'd never noticed before. There're cracks in the corners of her eyes, eyes that hold a wisdom many years beyond the young woman I've seen all this time.

"I'm thirty-eight, my love. You're only two years older than me."

"You're thirty-eight. Our daughter is twenty-two." I echo. Blue smiles, thin lines I'd never seen before framing her mouth.

"Yes, I was sixteen when I had her. Do you remember those fantasies you used to tell me about? The ones about us being best friends, neighbors, growing up?"

"Yeah, and the friends I'd made up, the fake memories I made to fill the emptiness."

"A lot of that was true, though. You really were my first. We were neighbors. We weren't in the same grade in high school. But we took the same college classes together later on, when Angel was older. And we got married when I turned eighteen."

"Angel, what about her? She was about ten last I saw her. I know she was."

"She used to come see you in the beginning. But as she got older, it got too hard for her. You saw her last the day she left for Africa two years ago. She joined the Peace Corps. I think she just needed to get as far away as she could for a while. She always hated how you treated her like a child. I don't know why I never figured it out, how you saw her as your little girl. Your mind must not have been able to cope with seeing the young woman she's grown into."

Is that possible? Could I really have been denying myself what was right in front of me all this time? I'd heard accounts of the first firefighters who responded to the scene of 9/11 who claimed to see piles of dead cows, and it wasn't until later they realized their minds couldn't cope with the reality of the human bodies they had seen. Was my mind protecting itself from the shock of the truth to prevent another...seizure-not-seizure...whatever it was, from happening again? Or could I simply not cope with the idea of having a daughter in her twenties—the age I thought I was?

"Alie—Black, hey, look at me." Blue—Natalie—shakes me. "Talk to me. You're too quiet. It's scaring me."

Alarm twists her features. The fear she must have felt revealing what little she would tell me at a time. The pain knowing I was but a shell with no memory of her, of our daughter. Yet she stayed by my side.

17. Old and New

"Why didn't you give up on me? Why fight so hard? I'm not the man who married you, who fathered our daughter. I'm something else. Something left over." I stare at my hands and wonder—ten years ago, were they callused from hard labor? Polished and manicured for some posh sales job? Did they teach Angelica anything? Or were they cruel to her? Who was I that Blue would fight this hard to recover?

"That's not true. You're so much like you once were. We may not be able to share our old inside jokes or reminisce our favorite anniversary getaways, but we can make new memories together. You're just as sweet and caring as you used to be. You may not remember everything, but even the way you hold me and kiss me is the same. You're you, you're still you. How can you ask me—how can you even think I'd give up on you?" Blue takes my hands in hers, splaying our fingers and lining up our palms. Her hands so very tiny against mine. "You'd do the same. We're each other's everything."

I would do the same for her. And more. But would the old me? I know only that this me, this present me would do anything for this present her. Was I so devoted before the accident? Did I take her for granted or cherish her?

"Tell me about your childhood home, Black."

"I don't—"

"Just try. Tell me about the one in your fantasies of us. What did it look like? What did my house look like?"

"Our bedroom windows faced each other. Our houses were closer together than any other houses in the neighborhood. You had a big inground pool we would hang out by all summer. My house was brown brick, yours yellow siding." As I detail my daydreams, her eyes crinkle at the corners.

"Come with me." I'm led from the playground. She parks the car in a spot then gestures I fall in step beside her. Thankfully left to my reeling mind, she asks no further questions as she leads me to some secret place with a smile on her face and her hand in mine.

It dawns on me on that walk. The feminine bedroom I was brought to with the lacy curtains. It was my daughter's bedroom. I wasn't brought to stay with Blue, I was brought *home*. To be with my *wife*. The man's clothes I saw in her closet and drawers one night as she slept were *my* clothes. I'd stood there holding a shirt against me, literally sizing up this missing husband and comparing him to my stature. I'd even slipped one shirt over my head and found the length just right but the fabric loose on my arms and torso.

In a way, I was wearing another man's shirt. The man before isn't me. I don't know any more about him than the reflection in the mirror. I feel like an imposter, an alien taking over this man's life. Somewhere buried deep within the confines of my subconscious mind, he must be pounding on the walls of his prison, begging to be set free, yearning to join his wife and daughter. But instead I've taken his place, a shell of a person who wears that other man's now aged face.

"Black, look." Blue squeezes my hand, drawing me out of the head that's not my head. We stand on the sidewalk facing my fantasy—no, facing reality. The houses from my daydreams! The brown brick, the yellow siding, the metal handlebar leading into what must be an inground pool in one backyard.

"It's...I don't—"

"They weren't fantasies, Black. They're your—our—memories."

I'm dumbstruck as I stare at reality and simultaneously into memory, not fantasy. Blue tugs me to follow her and I do on autopilot, mind overwhelmed and threatening overload. Breathe.

She kicks off her shoes, rolls up her pant legs, and dangles her feet into the water of the pool. "Join me." Blue pats the cement beside her. I glance back at the house, the windows still dark in the growing morning. It's still early, far too early for anyone on a Sunday.

"But the owners," I protest.

"They're elderly and sleep in pretty late. I like to walk by here sometimes on my own to do some daydreaming myself. Don't worry, even if they spot us, we can outrun them." She winks and I find my bared legs sliding in beside her.

"Your mom?"

"Ah, she moved to Cali to be with my dad after we finished college. Angel was still little. She would go and spend a few weeks every summer visiting them. We all went to visit once. I don't think you were a fan."

It's strange hearing details of old me's life and feeling no familiarity, no tingle of fuzzy memories as more and more of my past is revealed. I have so many questions now that I know the truth about us, the accident, and why Blue had been reluctant to tell me all this time.

"What did we go to college for? Did you get some kind of nursing degree?"

"Huh, nursing? Oh, I guess I shouldn't expect you to get up to speed so quickly. I'm not a nurse. Never was, never have been. If you saw me checking those machines and writing things down, it was for my own personal tracking. I don't know. I used to think the slightest spike in your heart rate or blood pressure were signs you were becoming more aware." Blue shrugs at this. Our feet sway idly in the water. "You went for a journalism degree, I forget what exactly now. You dabbled in the college newspaper before deciding it wasn't the type of writing you wanted to do. So you stopped going while thinking about a different degree and well, life got in the way."

"What did you go for?"

"Oh, right. I have an MBA. I was the supply chain manager for a farm feed chain for a while. They've gone out of business since I left. I've been doing consulting on the side for smaller companies since your accident."

My excitement about learning more diminishes. I never finished school. It sounds like I was a dreamer while Blue worked hard for us. Did I used to contribute anything? Was I deadweight? Have I always been a burden?

"So then, are we okay, financially?"

"Oh, stop worrying." Blue elbows me. The sparkling in her eyes shakes the darkness clouding my mind. "We're fine. I'm a damn fine consultant, if I do say so myself. And well sought after. There's actually a waiting list, y'know."

My shoulders relax at the truth in her words. But then an ache pierces my heart at the realization of how stupid I was to assume we were drowning in debt because of my medical bills. I nearly ended everything because of my selfish assumptions.

"Look, Black, I'm sorry. I should've talked to you, told you the truth a lot sooner. All this time, you must've been so worried about everything and I was too afraid to—"

"It's not your fault. What I was about to do...I'm so sorry." I pull her against me, breathing deeply into her hair. How I longed for this for years while my body remained stagnant. How could I have been about to throw this away when such love surrounded me? I'll never be able to repay her.

"I don't want to think about it anymore." Blue's somber words hold the faintest tremble. "What did you think was going on? If I was your nurse, you must've had some theories about what happened."

"Honestly? It was a tie between some weird obsession with your weakest patient and guilt because your husband was a drunk driver that caused my accident."

Blue snorts, pulls back to pin me with a look of disbelief, then erupts into a fit of giggles. Her laughter becomes contagious. "Wow. Okay, wow. Was not expecting that. Well, you were right about the drunk driver part at least. That'd make me a pretty bad nurse since I took advantage of my weakest patient." I'm nudged as a blush covers her cheeks.

"Or the best nurse, if you ask me." I nip at her neck, earning a little squeal.

"Pervert. Okay, what else do you wanna know?"

I think for a minute about the fantasy-memories; an old ache resurfaces thinking of a different time and a make up of a different kind in this very pool. "Did you kiss one of our friends to make me jealous years ago?"

"God, of course you'd remember that of all things." Blue throws her head back and laughs, a carefree sound. A lightness I hadn't noticed before seeps into my bones. Or is it a heavy weight leeching out?

"Was his name Colin?" I kick at the water, feeling the unfamiliar familiarity of this pool and this house and this meshing of fake me becoming real me, a mix of both, a little imaginary, a little made-new.

"No, Dustin was his name. Colins is my maiden name though, so in a way, I think you remember everything, just some of the details got a little mixed up."

"So you almost moved to California when your dad got some voice acting gig for a kids' movie?"

"Yup, and we ran away that night, thinking it would save everything. Come on." Blue stands abruptly, urging I do the same. Panicked, I glance at the house. It's still dark and quiet. "Let's go see if that island is still there."

And it is. The walk is so much shorter than I remember, the island so much smaller than I'd thought. The river more like a creek or stream. I trudge in.

"Hey, wait!" she calls from what could hardly be called the shore.

The water barely reaches my knees. I don't bother kicking off my shoes or rolling up my pant legs this time. A few long strides and I stand on the tiny rise in the center of the small stream. To think we thought we needed a blowup raft to get here when we were kids. That we believed this obvious out-in-the-open creek was a good place to run away is laughable now.

How easy it seemed to fix what felt like the end of our world as we knew it back then. If only an overnight spur-of-the-moment camping trip could solve adult problems. If only running away with Blue would always be the answer.

She waits for me, doesn't join me on the muddy island. I stare at the overgrown weedy dirt littered with plastic debris likely washed up with even a slight rain. If I could search hard enough, would I find any scrap of evidence that we were here, that it was real? A ribbon from her hair rotting around a branch, a petrified footprint, a tent stake rusting deep in the dirt?

I collapse against a tree and sink to the wet earth. The growing warmth of the day snakes around me, a heaviness in each breath. The sound of sobbing reaches my ears before I notice the trickle of tears streaming down my face. Blue smiles a sad smile, one that holds all that hope I'd nearly squandered. Like a child, I open my arms for her. *Pick me up, Baby Blue. Hold and coddle me.*

She runs through the water and into my arms, sinking into my embrace and melting into the mud with me. Sticks cling in her hair as I lay her exactly where our tent was once staked. I sink my hand into the cold dirt there, massaging it between my fingers before painting her cheeks with it. She smiles and, giggling, rubs mud onto my scruffy cheek.

"I love you," Blue whispers. She rips off one pant leg, kicking her clothing to one side, and, pulling my jeans down, she claims me on our tiny island. The sun forms a halo around her as she towers above me. The youth denied me absorbs into my skin. A trace of us, our past, our childhood, our hopes for the future, had all leaked into the dirt and sat waiting for us, for this moment. I feel it returning to me, a vigor restored, anticipation for tomorrow now mine.

"What now?" Muddied and glowing, we stride with new-found purpose back to the car. I stare at the passenger seat and contemplate stripping bare before soiling the light gray upholstery.

Blue laughs and plops into the driver's seat, grinding her muddy back into the chair. "Come on, get in!" Her laughter becomes infectious. "I hope it stains." She scrapes some of the mud from her cheek and rubs it into the fabric on the door panel, the grin never leaving her face.

18. Memoirs of a Missing Man

I walk through the door of my home with new eyes. Not-quite-memories tingle along my scalp. Ghosts of us curl up together for a movie in the living room. I see us cooking forgotten favorites in the kitchen, devouring the meals in our bed and sleeping in the crumbs. An awkward dance of our spirits try and fail at shower sex. Family hooky days and staying up too late and dessert for breakfast. Angelica interrupting sweet dreams to cuddle away her nightmares.

Each day, Blue shares details of us. Pictures of vacations. Concert stubs, field trip chaperone slips, all those souvenirs loving mothers and wives hoard in shoeboxes now splayed out on our bed. Perhaps the most surprising of the evidence that past me ever existed beyond that hospital bed is the laptop. A now dinosaur of a thing compared to the thin tech I see in movies and commercials. Folders and folders of stories and poems, journal entries, late night ramblings.

There were rejection and acceptance emails recovered with a stored password I'd otherwise never have remembered. I read through the accepted stories buried in small online magazines. I was a writer. Or trying to be. With whatever day job suited me to help make ends meet but a nightly focus to one day make it, Blue tells me. The largest document among them appears to be what was the beginning of my memoirs.

A haunting echo of myself reads the words to me. I can see the younger me, the one I thought I was in my fantasies, sitting in this chair, typing those words.

I don't remember meeting Lee. One day she was just there, filling a Lee-shaped hole I never remember being empty. We loved to play games, not board games or video games. But naughty groping drunken games. Games that crossed lines, and ultimately, hearts. It may be odd to start this story—my story—with love. But it's as true as these words. My story begins with love, Lee's love.

I read the opening chapter until the words blur and my throat tightens. They weren't daydreams. The memories truly were real, albeit muddled. The memoir stops mid-sentence. The chapter preceding it a detailing of some family disagreement that put tension between myself and my parents. Blue's persistence that we make up the reason for their trip. Even the last thing old me ever wrote was stopped short.

Mom and Dad will be here tomorrow. And I'll smile as I load their luggage, far too much for one week, into the trunk. We'll play pretend everything is all normal, ignoring the tension of things unsaid. And we'll be over it, the thing we won't talk about because my parents believe I love you means never having to say you're sorry. And that's okay. It's our way. It always has been but I—

But I what? Would old me, having the details of said argument, regret never truly making up before everything was over? Did it become my father's burden until his dying breath? My palms itch, the joints of my fingers ache. The keys begin to clack as my hands fly with knowing. Old me seeps into my body, a separation of two halves clicked and faded, overlapped.

I'll leave that last sentence unfinished. Because what happened next left the first part of this memoir truly and forever unfinished. I'm someone else writing this, someone new. I'm the same author but someone else. Allow me to explain.

Sweat breaks on my brow, a fever boils within me. I skip dinner as the words overtake me. This is it. Who I am now, who I used to be dying with each word. If a phoenix is cliché, then I am a dragon, roaring from the cinders with new purpose. I detail the first thing I remember, Blue running a rag down my arm. And I write without shame the shameful thoughts I'd clung to as I fantasized, no, reminisced about Blue.

I keep our nicknames, Black and Blue. A strange renaming of our characters in my personal cinema that becomes our born-again identities. Lee loves the nickname for its meaning and its source. I write out everything in a mad rush over the course of the next few weeks, desperate to lay it all out in fear that the memories I've discovered will leave me as quickly as they're named.

I detail amnesia and the strange ways it manifests beyond the falsities of the movies. As the memories are recognized, not returned in a sudden montage, but in a slow trickle of awareness, they never feel like mine. It's more that I become privy to details of old me's life as Alie living with Lee. But Black navigating this new life with Blue now reflects on those daydream memories like a spectator, not a participator.

An emptiness remains within me—I want to meet my daughter. But I'm too terrified to see the young woman standing where the little girl still stares at me with probing eyes. I fear it might break the fragility of the acceptance I have over the whole thing that is my life, new and old.

Blue suggests we start slow. A ten-minute phone call that is far too awkward to be real. Pictures of her growing up. I can't look at the rare pictures where I was present. It feels invasive, somehow. But it becomes too much to see her sad smile and all photos containing the obvious hole of my presence. It's as if my Angelica stood beside the ghost of me in every pose, a strange gap in every picture highlighting my absence. Her hand always outstretched as if reaching for me.

And I don't even remember her. Her birth, her first steps, her first day of school, her first words, her first "I love you" and "I hate you". How dare I ask for new memories, a new relationship if old me couldn't have bothered to daydream or reminisce the existence of his own daughter? Blue says to give myself a break. She thinks my memories only went so far, the rest yet to return to me. She's sure they'll come with time, with meeting my daughter again.

"HI, ANGEL'S DADDY. I'm Cole—Nicole. Nice to meet ya." The beautiful young woman outstretches her hand, and I wish more than anything memories would return to me so that I wouldn't have the awkward conversation of explaining that if we've met previously, I've no recollection of it.

"Hey, sweetheart! Dinner's almost ready. Come in, come in!" Blue ushers our mysterious guest to the table set for a surprise visit. I'll admit I'm a little disappointed Angel hadn't come home to fill that spot instead of this stranger.

"Black—that's what he likes to be called now," Blue says to this Cole Nicole woman. "This is Angel's fiancée. They met in the Peace Corps, isn't that right?"

"Actually, we met in college. We were both in a class where a guest speaker from the Peace Corps came to present and try to recruit volunteers. I stayed after to ask the teacher something about my grade and met her waiting to sign up."

Cole is captivating in that way where a model in a magazine holds your attention to the point you can't see the advertisement plastered around her. Deep, dark complexion, big shining eyes, thick voluminous hair. I want to ask her so many questions about my daughter, questions a father should know, questions I feel I have no right to know.

"What is it?" Cole dabs a cloth napkin to her lips with such fluid grace. My heart swells with pride and affection at knowing this woman, the fiancée to my daughter, would be joining our family. What little I do know of my daughter, she's clumsy and shy, bubbly bordering on awkward. This woman is her opposite yet perfect match.

"Sorry, I just...have so many questions."

Her eyes darken at my words, her brow furrowing with suspicion.

"Not like that. I mean..." I wonder if I can find a stray strand of Angel's hair woven through Cole's blue satin blouse. Would there be a hint of whatever perfume she wears still clinging to their furniture? Do they even live together? "Tell me everything."

Such love and warmth envelops her face as she tells of their shared life together. The break ups and make ups, the dealing with separation for so long, the brief stints of visits, plans for their wedding—postponed unknowingly for my sake.

"What time is it?" Blue suddenly interjects. After a glance at the clock on the stove, she quickly jumps up and leaves the room.

The ease of the dinner conversation cools at Blue's absence. She is the rock that helps me navigate this unfamiliar world. Without her, I find the next breath a struggle. Cole notices my discomfort and stammers to fill the silence with another story

"You know, we once got a dog together. One of those yippy little mop things chicks keep in their purses and tie up their bangs with bows. A dog with bangs? Not a dog, if you ask me. I had to pawn the thing off on a close friend not long after Angel left again. It's a real big, stinky dog or nothing for me, you know?"

I nod, knowing but not knowing.

19. New Memories

"Oh my God, you got rid of Princess?" I hear the most melodic voice in all of existence and something moves in my chest—a recognition, a claiming. My daughter. My Angel.

"Baby! I didn't know you'd be calling! I've missed you!" Cole jumps from the table to plaster her face in front of Blue's outstretched phone. A quick flash of her face appears before it's turned away from me. Blue's tentative smile wavers.

"Don't try to distract me, sweet pea. We're gonna have a nice long chat about this. Princess was our trail daughter, I'll have you know. You've failed mommy school and I haven't even been gone that long!"

"Yeah, yeah, yeah. Lecture me later. I know you didn't Face-Time to talk to me, not about no mop-rat anyway. You ready?"

Blue loops an arm around me, holding me steady. I hadn't realized I was shaking. I hadn't noticed I'd risen from the table and now stood behind the phone still turned away from me. My daughter. My daughter.

"Yeah," I answer, despite the question not being directed to me. Cole nods and turns the phone over. I'm terrified of it. What if I drop it, what if I break off the connection, end the face-call—whatever it's called, what if I see the disappointment and heartbreak in her gaze?

"Hi, Daddy."

Slowly, I open my eyes. My shoulders relax when I see the young woman and not the little girl I couldn't unsee before. My baby. I could feel the almost weightlessness of her in my arms, smell the wispy newborn hair as it tickled my nostrils. Not quite memories but a paternal recollection dances along my periphery. I see the toddler of her waddling to me, wrapping chubby arms around my legs.

She is the spitting image of her mother. But I also recognize myself in her. And my mother. Her face isn't Blue's heart shape but my mother's oval. Her lips aren't as plump as Blue's but more delicate, like mine. I'll bet she's tall with big feet, like me.

"Baby." My voice cracks. A monsoon of tears erupts all around. Blue, Cole, Angel, but my sobs are the loudest. I wail and cling to that phone, almost screeching as I apologize over and over. For everything. Missed birthdays, graduations, her first love and heartbreak, her last night in her home before venturing into adulthood without me.

She only has a few minutes. There's so much I want to say, to tell her and show her and ask her. What is the Peace Corps like, is she happy, does she hate me, when will she be home, does she hate me, when is the wedding now that I'm sort of back. God, does she hate me?

"Cole," Angel says through a sniffle.

"Yeah, baby. I'm here."

"Give it to him."

Cole leaves to retrieve something from her bag in the living room. And I struggle to find words that escape me the moment

I open my mouth. Before I can think of anything to say, Blue asks about some care package and if it'd arrived yet. I'm content for the moment just watching my baby's lips move around each syllable.

A thick notebook is held out to me. Cole smiles some sweet knowing smile as I stare down at it, afraid to grasp it, knowing that whatever it contains will break my heart and mend it and break it again.

"Don't be mad at me, Daddy. I wrote a lot of letters to you for years. They're all in that notebook. In almost every one, I promised to be a doctor and grow up to fix you."

"Oh, sweetheart, no one expected—"

"I know, Mama. I know. I just meant I'm sorry I made it sound like he needed to be fixed. I just wish sometimes I handled it all better. I should've been there to see him through recovery. I should've been there for you both. But I—"

"Don't, please." They're the first real words I've been able to utter. "Please, all of you. No more. No regrets, no apologies, no what-ifs or maybes. Just today. Just tomorrow. Just you, me, us. The past is gone. There's so much future now, we've no time to dwell. Baby, my Angel, thank you. I can't wait to read every word."

I DEVOUR EVERY CHILDISH scribble of grandiose promises and larger-than-life dreams, every teenage angsty letter, every young adult addition holding such regret and heartbreak. I add one of her letters to my memoir, much to her protest.

It's that letter I find myself reading over and over. The detailing of her career day at school, her promise to become a doctor and fix me. That part gives her the most regret, as she details in her letters when she got older. But it's heartwarming for me. I'd thought she'd have given up on me. That she must have hated me, wanted nothing to do with me, wished I had just died in the accident. But instead, she held hope all these years that we would play together again one day.

And as I stand here, palms sweating, body trembling, throat so damn dry, it's all I want too. She doesn't know it yet, but right after this, we're going to that playground. And we will play again. *I don't care if I'm fifty and you're one hundred, I wanna play again someday.* It may have been the wish of a child, and I may not be quite fifty, but I'll play on the playground with my daughter and fulfill that childhood dream.

"We're by the baggage claim. Are you almost here?" Cole is on the phone with Angel. I want to rip the phone from her hand just to hear my baby's voice. It's the first time I'll be able to hold her, to smell her, to feel the warmth and life of her. I'm not ready. What if the moment I see her, I have one of those convulsions that reset everything like what happened years ago? What if the pounding of my heart isn't excitement and anxiety but a heart attack just beginning?

"Hey." Blue's hand snakes in, lacing between my slick fingers. "Relax, Black. It'll be okay. You're ready. You'll be fine."

I look at her and see her for the first time all over again. This is Blue. Natalie. Lee. My wife. The mother of my daughter. The love of my life. With blue extensions in her hair—our own little inside joke that just so happened to look amazing on her—and her hand in mine.

"Thank you, Baby Blue." I kiss the top of her head and linger, breathing her in. She is a balm that soothes my frantic mind. And then she's running toward us, my daughter with tears down her beautiful face and a crowd of people scrambling out of her way.

"Baby!" Cole shrieks and runs into her arms. My heart starts pounding again. There's a clutching after their collision. A sinking of fingers into hair and a frantic mashing of mouths. Their lips move against each other's but the words are lost in the roar of the airport. It's such an incredibly touching scene but one I feel embarrassed to witness despite the fact I cannot avert my gaze away from her.

My daughter.

My Angel.

Cole steps aside, her hands to her throat, her eyes watering, watching me. And then Angelica is running to me. I have the strange urge to step back. Her mouth is open, her tongue moving. I see the words she screams but all sounds have silenced.

"Daddy, Daddy!" Angel launches into my arms, her legs wrap around me. And I'm holding my daughter. My adult daughter is in my arms and wrapped around me like a child. And the phantom of memory tugs, holding her like this, kissing her face, crying with her. I don't know when or why, but it all feels so familiar.

"My baby. My baby." I fall to my knees, clinging, clinging. Blue drops to her knees beside us, her arms tangling in.

I don't notice the crowd that has gathered to stare. I don't notice the pictures Cole is frantically taking that will be added to my memoir and also framed to line every wall of our home.

How fitting. This me, this mesh of old and new, of broken and mending, of whole in every other way. To be reunited with life in this airport, the one that over ten years ago set in motion the very fate that nearly ended me. My last visit here I led my parents to their deaths, a guilt I will carry until my dying breath. And now, I tremble on the floor of that very same airport, my wife, my daughter ensnared in my embrace. And the guilt lines with just a little bit of hope.

Blue drives, my fear of driving very much prevalent. We all continue sniffling, each of us taking turns to reach and touch any piece of Angel we can reach. A knee, a shoulder, her hair. Angel doesn't know we're on the way to the playground for a game of train. It will be awkward and ridiculous and exactly what we all need.

But Angel does know what I plan to do next. Blue didn't notice the little black box tucked in my pocket, or if she did, she must have assumed the jewelry purchase was a gift for Angel. And I got her something, too, but that comes later.

At the base of that slide, the playground of many daydream memories, of heartbreak and reunion, I plan to ask my Baby Blue to marry me. Again. We'll remarry on that little muddy island with Cole and Angel by our side. A wedding to fill the gap in my memory of our union twenty years ago.

The next few months will be filled with so many new memories to fill the gaps I hope will one day return. Cole and Angel's wedding is right around the corner. I'll get to see my daughter try on dresses. I'll get to walk her down the aisle. My heart swells at the incredible future laid out before me, at the new memories to be made, everything I almost threw away so thoughtlessly.

And it all begins as soon as Blue screams, "Yes!"

Thanks for reading!

If you enjoyed *The Drunken Promise*, be sure to leave a review! Reviews are very important and help authors and readers alike!

Want to connect?

www.Twitter.com/MaxWatsonBooks[1]

www.Facebook.com/MaxWatsonBooks[2]

www.Goodreads.com/MaxWatsonBooks

Want free stuff?

Check out my website www.MaxWatsonBooks.com[3] where you can sign up for my newsletter to get notified about new book releases, get free books, enter giveaways, be part of our book club and more!

---

1. http://www.Twitter.com/MaxWatsonBooks

2. http://www.Facebook.com/MaxWatsonBooks

3. http://www.MaxWatsonBooks.com

About the Author

Max Watson braves the sweltering heat of Dallas, Texas along with her husband Spencer, their son Jack, and their three kitty overlords. From roofing, to flipping houses and businesses, to building race cars, to ladder-climbing in corporate America, Max Watson loves to jump from one challenge to the next. In her career working for the man, she frequently found herself enthralled by the human psyche and was always daydreaming twisted tales. Running away screaming from corporate America, she decided to tackle the itch just under the skin and begin her writing career.